LOVE'S PAWN

Borgo Press Books by VICTOR J. BANIS

*The Astral: Till the Day I Die * Avalon * Charms, Spells, and Curses for the Millions * Color Him Gay: Being the Further Adventures of That Man from C.A.M.P. * The Curse of Bloodstone: A Gothic Novel of Terror * Darkwater: A Gothic Novel of Horror * The Devil's Dance * Drag Thing; or, The Strange Tale of Jackle and Hyde * The Earth and All It Holds * The Gay Dogs: Being the Further Adventures of That Man from C.A.M.P. * The Gay Haunt * The Glass House * The Glass Painting: A Gothic Tale of Horror * Goodbye, My Lover * The Greek Boy * The Green Rolling Hills: Writings from West Virginia (editor) * Kenny's Back * Life and Other Passing Moments: A Collection of Short Writings * The Lion's Gate * Love's Pawn (as "Victor Jay") * Moon Garden * The Pot Thickens: Recipes from the Kitchens of Writers and Editors (editor) * San Antone * The Second Tijuana Bible Reader (editor) * Spine Intact, Some Creases: Remembrances of a Paperback Writer * Stranger at the Door: A Novel of Suspense * The Sword and the Rose: An Historical Novel * This Splendid Earth * The Tijuana Bible Reader (editor) * The WATERCRESS File: Being the Further Adventures of That Man from C.A.M.P. * A Westward Love: An Historical Romance * The Wolves of Craywood: A Novel of Terror * The Why Not*

LOVE'S PAWN

Victor J. Banis Writing as

VICTOR JAY

THE BORGO PRESS

MMXII

LOVE'S PAWN

FIRST BORGO PRESS EDITION

Published by Wildside Press LLC

www.wildsidebooks.com

DEDICATION

I am deeply indebted to my friend, Heather, for all the help she has given me in getting these early works of mine reissued.

And I am grateful as well to Rob Reginald, for all his assistance and support.

CONTENTS

CHAPTER ONE

It was only a few weeks after his new stepfather Carl had moved into their house that the trouble began for Lenny Adams.

Lenny was in his mother's bedroom on some errand he forgot afterwards, and he stopped and stared about him at the new evidence of Carl's presence in the house—the clothes scattered about, a pair of cuff links on the dresser, a beer can beside the bed. He didn't know exactly how he got the urge, or why, but suddenly he wanted to see all of Carl's things, open the drawers of the dresser and see what horrible secrets might be hidden there.

In the first drawer he saw nothing but a few shirts and some undershorts, and he was feeling silly and even a little guilty by the time he opened the second drawer. He poked half-heartedly at a pile of socks, and saw the corner of a photograph. Almost without interest, he pushed the socks aside and picked up a stack of photographs. He stared at the top one, his mouth hanging open, and then looked at one or two more. They were pictures of men and women, doing things he had seen Carl and his mother do, and a great deal more. They were all of them naked, their bodies unashamedly exposed to the camera, and the acts they were performing were things Lenny had heard talked about by other youngsters, but had never seen before, even in photographs. Some of the pictures were of men with women, but some of them were of two or more men together!

He pushed the drawer slowly shut, holding the photographs tightly in his hand, and hurried back to his own bedroom, closing the door after him. His mother and Carl were out—his mother had gone to the doctor for a check-up, and Carl had gone out a short time before.

Lenny lay on his bed and looked at the pictures, staring long and hard at each one. He ran his fingers slowly over the surface, half expecting to feel the touch of naked skin. He tried to imagine himself in those pages, but it was too foreign to his experience, and the image wouldn't come. His body, however, responded to the efforts, and Lenny was aware of a growing rigidity, almost deliciously painful, in his loins.

He didn't know when Carl had come in, or how long he had been standing there in the doorway. He happened to glance up once, and there he was, his lips under the mustache curled into an ugly grin, black eyes glittering strangely.

Lenny jumped to a sitting position, the pictures scattering as he dropped them from his hands. He stared at Carl in wide-eyed fright, not knowing what to expect in the way of punishment.

Carl chuckled and came toward the bed, seating

himself beside Lenny. Automatically Lenny cringed from him, but the bed was small, and he was afraid to stand and move away.

"You like the pictures?" Carl asked, his eyes boring into Lenny. "Pretty hot, ain't they?"

When Lenny didn't answer, he chuckled again, picking up one of the pictures. He held it in front of Lenny. It was a picture of a man and a woman on a sofa.

"Ever do this sort of thing?" Carl asked. His breathing was strangely heavy and rapid, his nostrils flaring wide with each breath.

"Come on now, don't kid me." Carl had moved still closer, resting one hand on Lenny's knee. "A good looking young stud like you, don't tell me you're a cherry."

Lenny wanted to tell him that he didn't even know what the term meant, but he was afraid to speak. Carl's arm had gone about his shoulders, holding him close, and the hand on his knee was gently stroking the leg through the fabric of the jeans.

"What do you do, play around with fellows?"

"No!" Lenny almost shouted the word, horrified at the suggestion. He tried to pull away, but Carl held him firmly close.

Carl only laughed again at the boy's embarrassment and shock. "Nothing wrong with that," he said, his voice dropping lower. "You oughta try it."

The hand on his knee had begun to move slowly upward. Lenny felt his stomach turning as he realized what Carl was leading up to. He sat frozen with terror, trembling in Carl's arms.

"Now take me, for instance," Carl went on, almost whispering now as his face came closer to Lenny's. "I like a nice tender young boy every once in a while— good for a man's constitution."

He was pushing Lenny firmly backward, down against the surface of the bed, and Lenny felt the hand on his trousers, opening the buttons. He started to cry, trying in earnest to free himself from the embrace.

His efforts only amused Carl all the more

The hands became bolder and more insistent. "Hey, you got spirit after all," Carl whispered hoarsely.

Lenny blushed scarlet with shame as his body was laid bare by the demanding hands. His jeans were being pulled off him, leaving him naked and helpless. He saw, through tear-filled eyes, the loathsome sight of Carl's own body. Carl's face loomed over him, and Lenny smelled the stale beer and the odor of cigarettes as the mouth found his, the tongue forcing itself into his mouth and choking him.

He struggled wildly, but to no avail. He was no match for the full grown man, and he felt himself being twisted into position, viciously handled.

A lightning bolt of pain shot through him, seeming to split his body in two, and a hand clamped tightly over his mouth to stifle the scream of pain that rose in his throat. The pain grew, surging up within him again and again. Carl's breath was loud in his ear, and he knew that it was too late now to struggle.

He lay in an agony of physical pain and mental shame until it was over, barely fighting back the nausea as Carl's motions became more rapid and more violent until finally, with a gasp of delight, Carl convulsed violently again and again.

CHAPTER TWO

Things were never right for Lenny Adams. For as long as he could remember, life had never been anything but a contest to see who could screw who the first and the roughest.

Some kids could look back on their childhood with pleasure and remember it, or at least imagine it, as a time of pleasure hours and happy fun. Not so with Lenny. He remembered his mother, a nagging selfish woman who hadn't cared in the least for anybody but herself, whose only concern was her own comfort.

He couldn't remember his father too clearly, although he hadn't been all that young when his father had gone. From what he did remember, his father had been a nice enough guy, quiet, never angry, patient as anything. He had to be patient to live with the woman he had for a wife. Lenny couldn't bring his father to mind without picturing his mother too, following the little man around, nagging him, telling him how worthless he was, and yelling that she needed more money to keep the house. The last must have been a real joke— the house was never kept. As a very small child, Lenny had been made to take care of the dishes and keep things picked up, and the house-cleaning that he did daily under his mother's supervision was about all that ever got done.

Lenny might have liked his father, but there was never much opportunity for the two of them to get to know each other without the presence of the nagging, shrewish woman who turned everything into an ordeal. And then one day Lenny's father left. There wasn't any explanation of it so far as Lenny was concerned. His father didn't come home for dinner one night, and when Lenny mentioned it, his mother told him bitterly that he wouldn't be coming home again ever.

When he got a little older, Lenny gradually understood that they had separated, and that they were divorced. For a full year, he waited hopefully for his father to come back, not to stay, but to take him away also. He could not believe that a man as gentle and calm as his father could leave him there to suffer alone. But his father never came back for him, and after a time Lenny's fervent desire dimmed and became instead a deep seated bitterness toward the man who had abandoned him, and eventually toward all men. Men, it seemed to him, were a weak and worthless lot, not fit for anyone's affection. As for women, they were a race of vicious, bitter animals to be dealt with by whatever means.

He knew that his mother saw men, plenty of them, and he had acquired enough knowledge in the alleys of their dreary neighborhood and from the conversation of other boys to know exactly why she was seeing them and what was going on behind the closed doors of her bedroom. He avoided all men like the plague, hating them all with the same intense hatred he felt for his mother. That one of them might become a permanent fixture in the household never entered his mind until his mother introduced him to Carl.

"Kid, I want you to meet Carl," she announced one afternoon, placing herself in the doorway to block Lenny's intended departure from the house. "You'd better be nice to him, he's gonna be your old man."

Lenny jumped almost a foot off the floor and stared in open astonishment at his mother. This was something he had never suspected might happen, although he knew that people did get married more than once.

He forced himself finally to look past his mother at the man standing behind her.

Carl was a far cry from what his father had been. They were both quiet types, but there any similarity ended. His father's quietness had been the solitude of an unhappy but long-suffering man, and his father had never been anything but a simple creature of hard work and few needs.

Carl appeared to Lenny at once as the sort of man who was the villain in the cheap movies he sometimes saw, a thin, gaunt man with shrewd features and little eyes that darted about constantly, observing everything that went on about him. A narrow, shiny mustache added a sinister note to the dark, tight mouth.

"Pleased to meet you," Carl had told him, extending a hand toward Lenny.

Lenny took the hand silently, but he knew as he met those black, cold eyes that Carl's kindness toward him was only an act, an automatic device to assist him in getting whatever he wanted out of people.

"I've heard a lot about you," Carl was saying, and Lenny was uncomfortably aware that Carl was still holding on to his hand, the moist fingers clenching his own tightly.

"The kid's anti-social," his mother said, with a hoarse chuckle. "Don't worry about him, he's no trouble."

Carl let go of his hand finally, and Lenny seized the first opportunity to escape from the house and the two of them together. He didn't like Carl Jacobs, and the thought of sharing a house with the man was almost terrifying. He even thought of running away, but the big city offered no hospitality to him. He had no money, and no way of making any, and he was too afraid of strangers to plunge out into a city full of them.

Carl moved in a few days later, and Lenny never knew if the man and his mother had actually gotten married or not, nor did he care. The man was always in the house, watching Lenny as he came in and out, his eyes always following the boy until Lenny felt like a piece of food being devoured by the hungry eyes. Carl would show up at any time, in any place.

He cared nothing for Lenny's instinctive desire for privacy or his shyness. Lenny would be taking a bath, and the door would open and Carl would come in. Sometimes Carl would use the bathroom, making no attempt at modesty, and sometimes he would just stand by the tub and stare down at Lenny until Lenny wished that he could sink under the water and just disappear.

If Carl would decide that he was in a romantic mood, he would ignore Lenny's presence altogether while he made the overtures to Lenny's mother. Once, while Lenny sat across the room staring open-mouthed over the top of a book he was reading, the man opened his mother's blouse. Lenny felt a wave of nausea as his mother's huge, flabby breast came into view, but he watched with horrified fascination at what Carl did right there with him watching.

And *now*, Lenny thought, his eyes filled with bitter tears of pain and humiliation, Carl had raped *him!*

He was only half conscious of the fact that it was over. He heard Carl get up from the bed, but he lay where he was as though dead.

"Don't say anything about this to your old lady, okay?" Carl said finally.

Lenny opened his eyes, his anger coming to life again. "You know I will," he snapped fiercely.

Carl smirked viciously as his hand went into his pocket. The hand emerged holding a knife. There was a click, and the blade gleamed wickedly in the light. "I don't think you will," he said, stooping over Lenny again. Lenny said nothing. For a brief moment he met Carl's eyes, then he looked away, defeated.

"That's better," Carl said with a small laugh, closing the knife. His hand came back to Lenny's leg. "Besides, I like you. You and I can have a lot of fun together."

Lenny shuddered beneath the hand. "Don't worry,"

Carl went on, stroking the leg brazenly. "It's always rough the first time, but you'll learn to like it, you'll see."

From that time on, Lenny was never safe from Carl's twisted desires. He never knew when Carl might appear in the room, sometimes waking him from his sleep in the middle of the night. The man was insatiable, and the more Lenny fought against him or suffered from the acts, the more pleasure Carl seemed to derive from them.

After a time a merciful numbness began to develop in Lenny's mind, and he ceased to care. It was something that happened from time to time to his body, something he no longer cared about.

It was several weeks later that Carl brought a friend home with him one afternoon. Lenny's mother was out, and Lenny had thought himself safe from any disturbance. He had just finished a bath, trying to find some comfort from the afternoon's sultry heat. He was lying across his bed wearing nothing but a pair of jockey shorts, lazily reading a book when he heard the front door open and close.

His first thought was that his mother and Carl had returned home together. The footsteps were almost to his room before he realized that it was not a woman with Carl, but another man.

They appeared in the doorway before he had time to get up from the bed or cover himself. The man with Carl was fat and aging, an unattractive hulk of a man who seemed to overpower the room as he entered it.

"This is him," Carl was saying to the fat man. "Lenny, this is Joe. Joe wanted to meet you."

Lenny felt a new wave of revulsion as he recognized the expression on Joe's face. Joe was staring brazenly at him, his wide eyes moving hungrily up and down the length of exposed body.

"Why don't you two get acquainted," Carl was saying. He was already backing out of the room, pulling the door closed behind him. His eyes met Lenny's, and the warning in them was obvious. His hand patted the pocket which held the ever present knife.

"You're very nice," the fat man said when Carl had gone. He moved slowly toward the bed, his eyes glued to Lenny's jockey shorts.

Lenny closed his eyes, fighting off the fury that threatened to explode within him. Someday Carl would pay for this—*someday the whole rotten, stinking world would pay for the way he had been made to suffer.*

The fat man was with him on the bed. Damp, eager hands tugged at the cloth around Lenny's hips, and automatically, like a machine, his body responded. He had learned well from Carl, he knew just what to do and how to do it, and despite his hatred and the fact that there was no pleasure in it for him, he provided his partner with the maximum delight. He didn't even bother to open his eyes afterward when the fat man got up, wheezing, dressed and left the room.

After that, there was not only Carl, but an increasing string of strange new friends that he brought home with him whenever the mother was out. They were a widely mixed assortment of men, some young, some old, some ugly and some not so ugly, but they all shared one thing in common—their undisguised lust for the sexual pleasure his body offered them.

It was weeks later before Lenny discovered what was going on. One of the men had just finished with him, and was beside the bed, dressing. Lenny was staring at him with blank eyes that gave no clue of his feelings, and wondering what made such animals of men, what drove them to the limits that they had reached.

The man finished dressing and looked down at him. "Who do I give the money to?" he asked in a business-like tone.

Lenny's eyes widened slightly. "Money?" he repeated, puzzled.

The man stared at him for a moment before a look of comprehension came over his face. "Oh, I get it," he said quietly. "Forget it, okay."

The man left, and Lenny heard him talking to Carl in the hall outside. He lay on the bed and thought back over the past weeks. Money, of course. These men weren't Carl's friends, they were customers, and *he* was the merchandise Carl was selling. While he had been on this bed, satisfying the desires of all these strangers, Carl had been pocketing the money that they paid for their brief time with him.

Carl came into the room a short time later. He grinned at the expression on Lenny's face. "So he told you about the money," he said slowly.

"They've been paying *you* to shack up with *me*,"

Lenny snapped, too angry now to care about the knife or Carl's threats. "And you never told me about it."

"Okay, okay," Carl said with a wave of his hand. "Don't let it get to you. Look, there's no reason why we can't both make a profit out of this. You got a right to a little spending money, so I'll split it with you."

He took his billfold out of his pocket and pulled out two one dollar bills, tossing them to the bed. "They give me five bucks. You get two of it, okay?"

Lenny knew that he had no real choice in the matter. But he had another reason, too, for nodding his head finally. The money. He had never had any money of his own and this was his chance to make some. Maybe eventually *he* could even earn his freedom from Carl. At any rate, he knew that he would have to continue enduring the procession of men coming in and out of his bedroom—he might as well be making some money while he was at it.

"Just one thing," he said. He had grown hard and bitter during his time with Carl, and he knew that the value of his body could be an effective tool for handling Carl. "If we're going to make a business of this, let's keep it a business. Every time you come in here to see me, you're throwing away that much money we could be making off of me. Okay?"

Carl was surprised, and for a moment Lenny expected him to become angry, but he thought about it for a moment and finally laughed again. "You're right at that. I'll have to hand it to you, you're a smart little kid."

After that Carl didn't bother him. His greed proved to be more powerful than his lust. But if Lenny had expected to gain any freedom or rest for himself, he had been mistaken. Carl had taken him at his word, and the time that he had previously spent with Lenny was given over to new customers.

If Lenny was no happier than in the past, at least he was making a little money now, and his hoard was growing slowly but steadily. There were many times, he was sure, when Carl was paid more than the five dollars, but he didn't risk the chance of asking about it. He took his two dollars each time and added it to what he had in the tin can under his bed. With the knowledge of his sexual power and the hold that it gave him over men, his shyness was quickly vanishing, and in its place was an arrogant disregard for anything and anybody. The world existed for him to get what he could out of it.

It was inevitable that his mother would find out eventually. Lenny didn't know how it had been possible to keep things as they were for so long without her finding out. He considered it likely that she was spending her time making money in much the same way, and more than likely Carl was managing her business just as he was managing his own.

She came home one afternoon while Lenny was with one of Carl's friends. Lenny felt the man in bed with him tense and jerk away. He opened his eyes and looked toward the door, to see his mother standing there, staring at them. She turned and walked away from the door.

When the man had left, his mother came in again, standing in the doorway with a cigarette dangling from her mouth, her voice and face emotionless. "Carl tells me you two been making a little spending money for yourselves," she said.

"Why not," Lenny answered her with a calmness that belied his true feelings. "It's not a bad racket."

"You got no beefs?" The question impressed him as a strange one, coming from her. He wondered, almost idly, if she were for the first time trying to express a motherly interest in him. More likely, he concluded bitterly, she was thinking about the legal risks.

"No beefs," he told her curtly. He reached for the pack of cigarettes on the dresser, and lit one. This was another habit.

She shrugged, and left without saying anything more. After that they didn't concern themselves with whether she was in or out of the house, and business picked up steadily.

No beefs? The hell he didn't have any beefs! He'd been taken advantage of by his stepfather and by all the vile male creatures who'd come lusting into his bedroom.

It was time, Lenny decided, to start taking some advantage for himself!

CHAPTER THREE

Before long, Lenny had become highly skilled in his trade. His looks had ripened into full bloom, and the prices that Carl asked for him had risen accordingly. Lenny's cut was five dollars now, and Carl kept the other five or ten for himself. The tin can under the bed had been replaced by a strongbox, and occasionally Lenny would take some of the money and spend it on new clothes or something for himself.

His youthful good looks also attracted girls, and Lenny was pleased that he was just as virile and physically contented with them as with his male customers. However, his female conquests were few and far between. He had all the sex he could manage right at home, and sex to him meant money. He had neither the desire nor the inclination to reduce his earning power by wasting it on sex for pleasure.

He had learned a great deal besides the art of sex. He had learned to talk to his customers, and from them he had acquired a certain rough polish. He knew how to dress, a little about manners and social niceties, and he wore a veneer of good taste that only added to his rugged charm.

He stood almost six feet, with a body that was slender but magnificently chiseled as though from fine stone. He had discovered that his looks were his big asset, and he saw to it that they were accorded the respect they deserved. He held rigidly to his insistence of a full night's sleep, good meals, and time enough during the day for a period of working out. His arms rippled with muscles, his wide shoulders tapered to a slim waist and hips. With age the natural equipment that he possessed had grown into a treasure of splendid proportions.

He had begun, too, to supplement his regular earnings. While the men who came to see him were on the bed with him, or in the bathroom, their clothes were harmlessly draped on a chair across the room. Lenny glanced in that direction one afternoon, his eyes coming to rest on the bulge of a wallet in one pocket. From then on, the chair stood next to the bed, close enough that Lenny could reach it with one hand. He began regularly to help himself to a "tip" from each visitor, being shrewd enough to take amounts that he thought would not be noticed. If the wallet was filled with bills, he was generous with himself. If there were only a few there, he limited himself to one, or maybe two dollars.

His conscience, if he even had one, gave him no trouble. This was a business to him, and he had every right to make all that he could off of it. As for the customers, they were only so many dollar signs to him.

Sooner or later it was bound to occur to him that Carl was making an easy living off of him. He was doing the work, sweating and panting on the bed with countless men, and Carl was pocketing a lion's share of the profit.

He no longer had to fear Carl. He was taller than his step father, and formidable in appearance. Even the knife in the pocket wouldn't give Carl the courage to stand up to him. There was only one thing that he needed, Carl's knowledge of picking up customers.

"I want to go with you," he said one day when Carl was getting ready to leave the house.

"What for?" Carl asked, shooting him a suspicious glance.

"It gets kind of tedious, laying on that bed all day," Lenny told him, making it apparent that his mind was made up. "And besides, I think I should know a little more about the business."

Carl relented begrudgingly. He had no choice, after all, although he was shrewd enough to suspect what Lenny was leading up to.

In all this, as well as in sex, Carl was a good teacher, and Lenny was a good student as well. He accompanied Carl to the bars and parks where he made his contacts. He learned how to spot a prospect, and how to approach him, how to decide which ones were likely to be vice, and which ones weren't worth wasting the effort on.

At first Carl had no reason to object. The prospects could see what they were getting, and Lenny's youthful good looks, coupled with the air of innocence he learned to assume, increased their volume steadily.

The day came soon enough when Lenny felt that he was ready to move ahead on his own. He had learned all that he could from Carl, and from here on in Carl and his mother were just so much dead weight for him to carry around.

It was easy enough to get them out of the way. It took an anonymous call to the police, and a few days later the customer that Carl took home to his mother proved to be a vice officer. They were arrested, while Lenny stood across the street, out of sight behind a parked car, and watched them taken from the house. He was on his own, now, and ready to start moving.

He spent a day or two just loafing, enjoying his new freedom. Carl called once from the jail to ask Lenny to put up the money for bail and get a lawyer for them. Lenny promised he would, and promptly forgot about it when he had hung up the phone.

The second night, he decided that he was ready to go to work. He cleaned up, carefully shaving the hint of a beard that had begun to appear on his face. He picked his clothes carefully—tight fitting slacks that showed off the enticing contours of his buttocks and the impressive bulge in front. With a clean tee shirt, a sweater, and sneakers, he looked like the typical football hero—or nearly so.

He spent half an hour combing his hair, creating just the right effect of youthful abandon. Then, satisfied finally with his appearance, he left the house and set out for the park he had chosen as a starting place.

It didn't take long. He hadn't walked halfway through

the darkened path before he was being followed. He turned off the path, heading for an area of darkness and trees where they would be unseen by passersby, and sized up his prospect with one quick glance. The man was in his thirties, nicely dressed in a conservative suit and tie, a little nervous as he hurried along in Lenny's wake, following him off the path. Lenny flashed him a knowing smile to seal the bargain, and led the way further into the darkness, pausing finally at a clump of bushes.

The stranger approached slowly, giving Lenny a timid once over. The gleam in his eye was evidence that he liked what he saw.

"Nice night, isn't it?" he said, coming to a standstill.

"For some things," Lenny answered. He dropped one hand to his thigh and rubbed meaningfully. "You buying?"

"Ten dollars," Lenny told him simply. He waited for the man to nod before he stepped back into the bushes, legs tensed, his hand tugging the zipper of his slacks downward.

As the stranger feverishly sought the pleasure that Lenny's firm young body had promised, Lenny waited patiently, moving skillfully, judging when the man had gotten his money's worth before allowing himself to reach completion.

They stood, readjusting their clothing. Lenny waited for the man to take his wallet from his pocket before reaching out one hand.

"I'll take that," he said coldly. He was free of Carl

now, free to operate as he wanted, and had no intention of settling for chicken feed any more.

The stranger stared at him with an expression of fear in his eyes. "You said ten dollars," he whined, but he offered no resistance as Lenny took the wallet from his hand.

"So?" Lenny went through it quickly, taking all the money and cramming it into his pocket. "Call the police, why don't you. They might want to know what you were doing here in the bushes with a minor."

The man swallowed, and said nothing. Lenny tossed the wallet to the ground, and looked over his companion again. "Give me the watch," he snapped. "The watch, right now," he said coldly when the man started to protest.

He took the watch and a tie pin that looked like a diamond. Not bad for twenty minutes work, he concluded, dropping them also in his pocket. He lifted his eyes to the stranger. *It wasn't just one man standing in front of him, helpless and frightened—it was all the men who had used him and squeezed the life from him*—the father who had disappointed him, Carl raping him mercilessly, all of the others coming in and out of his bedroom. His fist shot out like a bolt of lightning.

The man's cry caught in his throat and became instead a flow of blood that gushed from his mouth. Lenny hit him again and again, driving him to the ground. His fists and his feet rained blow after blow on the helpless figure writhing about in the grass.

Finally, his anger relieved, he left the man lying unconscious in the grass and strolled calmly away, his eyes studying the park about him, looking for another prospect.

CHAPTER FOUR

He never saw Carl or his mother again. By the time they had gotten out of jail, Lenny had taken a place of his own, a nice little apartment in a slightly better neighborhood, but one where he would have maximum privacy and a minimum of questions asked.

He was free now to live as he wished, and he had set definite goals for himself. He had seen, in his own experience and in working with Carl, that a little class went a long way. Right now his youth was his chief asset, but he would not always be able to depend on that, and he set about learning the niceties of being a gentleman. He visited the better bars and restaurants, sometimes plying his trade, sometimes playing the role of a perfect gentleman. He took time out from work to date girls, and had no problem finding girls who would go out with him or who would permit him to take the sexual liberties he demanded of them.

In his trade, he had become a ruthless brute. More often than not, when the sexual play was finished, he would leave his customers beaten and bleeding on the ground. With almost no exceptions, he took with him all the money they had on them, and any other valuables they possessed. He had no feelings for any of them, and consequently no mercy. Besides, this way he made enough money from a few scattered encounters to meet his financial needs and leave the rest of the time free.

When he had worked one area for a while he would switch and begin working another, avoiding the risk of being seen again by one of his victims. He was footloose and fancy free, and he had every intention of staying that way.

When he chose, he was a handsome, charming young man perfectly at ease in any place or situation. When he was working, he was a savage beast of the night, a beautiful and bewitching young animal who would turn upon his victims with vicious ferocity. It never occurred to him to wonder if he was happy—he had never known what happiness was, and he had long ago ceased thinking of it. He was comfortable, his needs were met, he had the pleasure of sexual activity whenever he wished it, with a member of either sex, and the additional pleasure of being the master of his unfortunate prey. If anything, he derived his greatest satisfaction out of seeing people helpless before him, a slave to his wishes.

And then one night he made a mistake.

Instinct told him as he watched the man approaching him where he stood near a tree that something was not quite right, but he dismissed the thought and made the customary advances. He should have realized the truth when the man continued to stand, ignoring the invitation to kneel in front of him.

"Don't you want it?" Lenny asked with a smug smile, still not comprehending.

"Not particularly," the stranger told him.

Lenny wasn't thinking clearly, or certainly he would have seen the writing on the wall. All he was thinking of, however, was that he needed some money, and the man before him no doubt had some on him.

"Look, I need money," he said quickly, reaching out one hand toward the stranger. "I'll take what you've got, and don't give me any trouble."

"Oh?" the stranger stepped back a step, giving Lenny a funny little smile.

"I warned you not to give me any trouble," Lenny snarled, coming after the man. To his surprise, this one didn't cringe, or fall apart as the others did. This one swung, his fist landing soundly on Lenny's jaw.

Lenny swore and went for him again, and this time the stranger sent him tumbling on the grass. He stared up at the man, not believing what had happened.

"I think you'd better come along with me," the man said, and Lenny saw the badge for the first time.

He got off with a warning from the judge, and a week later he was back in business. Only a week after that he picked another vice officer. He didn't even try to cruise this one, just came up behind him in the park late one night and tried to put him out with a fast blow. For the second time it was Lenny who landed in the grass.

This time he went to jail. He learned a lot while he

was there, including some fine points in the plying of his trade. But jail did serve to reform him, in one sense. Rolling people in the park wasn't the answer, not because he felt guilty about it, but only because the risk was too great of getting arrested again. He was still determined to take what he could away from the world, but he had come to the realization during those months of being locked up that there were better ways than he had been using.

When he was released from jail, he had lost the look of childish innocence, although he still had a youthful quality about him. He was as hard all the way through as a keg of nails, and the hardness was hidden beneath an exterior that would have fooled almost anyone into believing him a saint.

The parole officer warned him to get a job, and that one more such arrest would be really rough on him. The latter wasn't worrying Lenny; he had already reached the same conclusion.

For the present, he decided that he would find a job, something to give him at least the appearance of being legitimate. Once that was accomplished, he would be free to start after what he was looking for—someone with the kind of money to keep him in style.

One of the boys in jail with him had told of his experiences. He had been kept by a wealthy dowager for two years, living in the lap of luxury with nothing to do for it but visit her bedroom once or twice a month. It was her sudden death in an automobile accident that had put him back on the streets and driven him to the robberies that had sent him to jail. But the prospect of being kept had impressed Lenny as a very nice one. He had everything necessary to make a success of such a role, including the charm, looks, and sexual abilities. All he needed was someone with a bankroll, and it didn't matter whether the person was male or female!

CHAPTER FIVE

It took Lenny a week before he found a job that looked promising. The AC-DC ELECTRICAL MANUFACTURING COMPANY had advertised for a man, and as soon as Lenny saw the woman who was to interview him, he knew instinctively that this was the place for him.

Gloria Denning was all anyone could ask for in a woman. Her shimmering blonde hair fell about her shoulders in cascading waves, framing a face that might have been in any fashion magazine. Her body, notwithstanding the simple business suit she wore, looked more like something from a pin-up calendar. Huge breasts jutted out sharply against the fabric of her outfit. A narrow waist swelled out into wide, curvy hips and flaring buttocks, all set atop the shapeliest legs Lenny had ever seen.

His first thought as he followed her into her office for the interview was that he wanted her sexually, if it were at all possible.

"You're the personnel manager?" he asked, seating himself across the desk from her. He was having a hard time trying to keep his eyes from the outlines of her breasts.

"No, she's off for the day. I'm Miss Denning," she told him, paying no apparent attention to his interested stare. "I own the company."

Lenny decided she was just what he had been looking for. For the moment, she was all business, and he couldn't tell if she was interested in him or not, but he had full confidence in his sex appeal and his ability.

He turned on the charm full blast, and pulled out all stops to get the job. He lied about his education, which was almost nothing except what he had learned on his own. He made up experience that was in line with the business of the manufacturing company Gloria Denning owned, using a natural flair for acting to make it all convincing. He even lied about his age, to make the rest of it seem logical.

It worked. He got the job, training as an assistant to Gloria Denning herself. He left her office with instructions to report to work the following day. His confidence and his spirits were soaring. Even the prospect of going to work seemed a grand one in his way again.

He was there bright and early the next morning. Miss Denning greeted him in a friendly enough voice, although she was still being strictly business, and showed him around the offices.

"This is Sylvia," Gloria told him, introducing him to a sharp looking young brunette. "She's my secretary, and she'll take care of things for you as well."

"Welcome aboard," Sylvia greeted him with a dazzling smile.

"Nice meeting you," Lenny said, smiling back. He wasn't exaggerating, either. He was only recently out of confinement, and there hadn't been much time to spend on sexual endeavors. He had forgotten the thrill of sexual interest. Working for the Denning Company was apparently going to be quite pleasant.

His job wasn't all peaches and cream. For one thing, he had built himself up pretty well to get the job, and he found himself faced with tasks about which he knew nothing. His quick mind and a strong determination had to carry him through until he could absorb enough knowledge of the business to manage the job properly.

He worked hard, and he had one other thing in his favor—Sylvia took to him right off, and she gave him all the help she could manage. Once or twice he caught her giving him funny looks, and he was sure she had guessed how little he really knew, but she held her tongue and worked all the harder for him. If he hadn't needed all his attention for the work, he might have made a real play for her, but he had other things on his mind for the moment. Later, when things were going more smoothly, he would work on that matter.

To his disappointment, he didn't see as much of Gloria Denning as he had hoped, and when he did it was always too brief to make much progress with her. She remained business through and through and although she was always pleasant and charming, there wasn't any sign that she had even noticed his looks or appeal.

He was sitting at his desk one morning, staring after

her as she moved across the office, her hips swaying enticingly, when Sylvia spoke from behind him, catching him off guard.

"That look should be reserved for stag movies," she told him.

He turned around, startled, and saw her grinning at him. He returned the grin and relaxed again. "Well, you have to admit, she'd be quite a catch."

"She would be," Sylvia agreed, going to her own desk nearby. "And was. Her husband no doubt thinks so."

"Husband?" Lenny rose half from his chair. "But I thought she...."

"...was single?" Sylvia grinned, plainly enjoying his astonishment. "Don't let the *Miss* Denning fool you, she only uses that for business convenience. There's also a *Mr.* Denning, and he isn't her father."

Lenny clenched his fists in front of him on the desk and stared off across the office. That was something he hadn't counted on. It was beginning to look as though his efforts had been in vain.

It was difficult for him to restrain his annoyance when Gloria Denning stopped at his desk a short time later. "I suppose you've learned that we're having a showing tonight," she said, lighting a cigarette from the pack on his desk. "I know you've scarcely had time to learn the business, but I think you might find it interesting if you come. It will be a good chance to meet some of the clients, and besides there'll be plenty of free drinks."

"Fine," he told her, his voice even despite the anger within him. "In fact," he added impulsively, "Maybe Sylvia will come with me."

He turned toward Sylvia's desk. "I'd love to," she accepted eagerly.

He had hoped that his invitation to Sylvia might produce some reaction on Gloria's part, but if it did she didn't let it show.

"Fine," she said, smiling at the both of them. "See you both tonight."

CHAPTER SIX

Lenny arrived early at Sylvia's apartment. He had begun to wish that he had declined the suggestion that he come to the showing, but there wasn't anything that he could do now to get out of it. Anyway, he consoled himself, things weren't all as bad as he had first thought. The fact that Gloria Denning was married wasn't an insurmountable obstacle. Women had gotten divorced before, and married women had been known to keep lovers on the side. Time would tell, and in the meantime he had a date with an attractive brunette, with all sorts of pleasant possibilities for the evening.

The possibilities presented themselves sooner than he had expected. Sylvia had obviously just finished her shower when he rang the doorbell. She opened it a moment later with a filmy negligee wrapped loosely around her trim young body.

"You're early," she told him, opening the door wide. "You'll have to make yourself comfortable while I finish dressing."

"Sure I can't help?" he asked in a low voice, moving close to her. She blushed as she read the message in his eyes, but she made no attempt to move away.

He came closer, one arm slipping about her waist. "There's something I've wanted to do for a long time," he told her, pulling her close. His face came down toward hers, his mouth seeking and finding her mouth.

It was like making contact with a live wire. She moaned and went soft in his arms. He could feel the warmth of her body through the thin fabric of her negligee. Sylvia, at least, would be easy enough. She was too hot for him to offer any resistance.

"It won't hurt if we arrive a little late," he told her, his own body growing warmer as his ardor began to rise. He moved back from her, slipping the fabric gently from her shoulders. It made a soft rustling sound as it fell to the floor at her feet, and she was naked before him.

His eyes took in the view. She was short and trim, with pert, young-girl breasts that jutted sharply before her. Her stomach, flat and taut, melted into creamy white thighs.

She was trembling. He pulled her to him again, kissing her heatedly. Her breasts were crushed against his body, the heat from them like a welding torch.

He picked her up easily in his arms and carried her to the open doorway and the bedroom beyond. She lay with her eyes closed on the bed as he stripped himself of his own clothes. He came to her quickly, kneeling over her, his mouth tracing its way over the softness of one breast. His hands stroked her thighs, slowly and skillfully playing upon her body like a fine instrument. Her passion was rising quickly, her body trembling and writhing beneath him.

"Oh, Lenny, Lenny," she gasped, clinging to him. "Take me, please, take me."

Her thighs welcomed him, her body shaking frantically as his joined with it. Her hips rose, eager for the delirious pleasure he was giving her.

He started slowly, deriving pleasure from the way she squirmed and twisted as though being tortured. Gradually he increased the tempo and the intensity of his movements, carrying her along with him, until their bodies were heaving and lashing wildly about on the bed.

It had been a long time since he had had a woman, too long. Even if he was incapable of any feeling for them, he could still enjoy the sheer physical joy of a woman's body softly yielding beneath his as Sylvia's was now.

Her fingers clawed at the bare skin of his back, seizing his buttocks as though to draw him into her totally. She bit at the flesh of his shoulder, moaning and whimpering as they raced wildly through time and space together, approaching the apex of their lust.

"Now, Lenny, now," she moaned, flinging herself wildly against him as her body convulsed frantically. With a small cry, he crushed her against the surface of the bed, giving himself up to a spine shattering climax that left him weak and panting.

Much later he rose and reached for her cigarettes, lighting one for each of them. "You're pretty great," he told her as he handed her the cigarette.

It was true. He had derived more pleasure from her than from any sexual experience in his past. There had been no money involved this time, and no ulterior motives, nothing but sheer passion, and he had given and gotten the ultimate pleasure.

He wondered, as she lifted her face upward to kiss him, how Gloria Denning would have been. His confidence in himself had been fully restored, and he was more determined than ever that he would have Gloria Denning, regardless of how he did it, or who got hurt in the bargain.

And in the meantime, he thought happily, there was Sylvia, her naked body pressed warmly against his, still hot and eager. Things weren't going so badly, after all.

CHAPTER SEVEN

It was fairly late when they finally arrived at the company show. The place was already filled with people, some of whom Lenny recognized as company people, and others whom he assumed were various clients and business associates. They got themselves drinks and stood at one end of the room, watching the crowds. Sylvia pointed out several people to him, particularly the more important clients, and gave him bits and pieces of information about them.

"And there's the boss lady," she said glibly, nodding across the room.

Lenny followed her glance and saw Gloria, looking stunningly beautiful in a clinging white sheath that made her look like anything but a business executive.

"The man with her," he asked after a moment. "Who is he?"

"That, believe it or not, is Mr. Denning, Nick to his friends." The way she said it caused him to give her a puzzled look.

"Well you have to admit," she said with a slightly malicious smile, "He's an unlikely type for her. He doesn't look like he's man enough to keep her happy."

Denny looked back at Nick Denning. She was right, at least partially. Sylvia was no great judge of character, and from his own experience he would have guessed Denning to be far more torrid sexually than she guessed. On the other hand, he didn't really seem the type for Gloria. He was scarcely taller than she was, slender and fair, nice looking in a rather plain way.

"What does he do?"

"He's a writer," Sylvia answered. "Rather a good one, I hear. The business was already hers when they met, and he's never had any real interest in it, so she's just continued to run it while he writes. If you ask me, he's more the sort to be in the ballet."

"What makes you say that?" Lenny asked, knowing full well what she was driving at.

"You know the type," she told him calmly. "Don't get me wrong, I'm not saying he goes that route, but I'd be willing to bet the right man could talk him into changing his way of life."

Lenny stared across the room at Nick Denning. She was right, of course, the possibility was there in him—not flagrantly so, not even so that Carl or Lenny would have considered him a prospect back in the days when he was cruising the parks. But it was there, and the right man could probably do a great deal with it.

It wasn't the answer he had been looking for, but her husband was a far more likely place to begin. Once he was out of the way, the path would be clear for him to move in. If he were married to Gloria Denning, he would never have to worry about making money again.

"I think you're mistaken," he said aloud. Sylvia was a good kid, but she wasn't bright enough to be of any help in his scheme, and he didn't want her catching on to what was happening. "Come on, we'd better go over and say hello at least."

They made their way across the crowded room, to where the Dennings were standing.

"Why, hello," Gloria greeted them cheerfully as they came up. "Nick, this is my new assistant, Lenny Adams. Lenny, my husband."

They shook hands, Lenny deliberately prolonging the gesture. He suppressed a smile as he saw Nick blush shyly.

"My wife's been telling me what an asset you are," Nick said quietly, finally pulling his hand free.

"I'm glad to see I'm not her only asset," Lenny said warmly, staring deeply into Nick's eyes. To his delight, he saw that the remark left the man all the more flustered.

"Well, if we're all finished throwing bouquets," Gloria said, "why don't you two join us for a drink?"

The meeting went well. Lenny was charming and pleasant, careful to direct as much of his attention toward Nick as was possible without making it obvious. Unlike Sylvia, he could understand the mating of Gloria and Nick—she was strong and domineering, Nick just the opposite, a quiet, reserved type who could be easily thrown for a loop. He was also certain, as the time passed, that Nick was being thrown for a loop at the present.

A short time later, Nick excused himself and left them to go to the restroom. Another group drifted by at the same time and a new conversation started up. Lenny waited until the conversation was safely under way and the attention off of him before excusing himself and walking away.

Nick was standing at one of the stalls when Lenny entered. Lenny saw the startled expression followed by a slight blush as Nick recognized him. He walked up to the stall beside Nick, exposing himself boldly. He didn't even have to look to know that Nick was staring at him.

They stood much longer than was necessary, Lenny deliberately prolonging the scene. He had been right, Nick was boiling over with potential that was only just below the surface. He was ripe for picking.

"Want to talk about it?" he asked abruptly.

Nick shot him a startled and embarrassed look. "What does that mean?" he stammered, caught off guard by the remark. He stepped away from his stall quickly.

Lenny chuckled and gave the benefit of a dazzling smile. "Don't be afraid," he said in a low voice. "I've been around quite a bit, you know."

"I don't know what you're talking about," Nick insisted, turning toward the washbasin. Lenny moved after him, standing close behind him. One hand went to Nick's waist, and he felt the body trembling as he pressed lightly against it.

"Oh yes you do," he said, leaning close to Nick's ear.

Their eyes met in the mirror, and Lenny knew that he had made his goal. Nick's face was a storm of emotions—fear, guilt, embarrassment, shock—but there was desire there too, too obvious to be ignored.

Lenny smiled at the face in the mirror before stepping back from the washbasin and leaving the restroom. Nick Denning, he told himself as he went back toward the group on the opposite side of the room, could be had, and Lenny was going to have him, very soon.

CHAPTER EIGHT

Lenny rejoined Sylvia and Gloria, slipping easily back into the conversation of the group. A moment later, Nick came from the restroom and made his way across the room toward them. Lenny could barely suppress a smile as he observed Nick's agitated manner.

Throughout the evening, Nick continued to be plainly upset, avoiding the necessity of looking at Lenny or even touching him. As for Lenny, he was enjoying the game that he was playing, and he played it to the hilt. He was flirtatious, charming, appealing, clever—all of this directed at Nick. The fact that he was torturing the slight, timid young man only made the situation more enjoyable than ever.

At the same time, Lenny was carefully steering the conversation of the group in the directions he wanted, gathering information that would be useful to him in his campaign. At one point he steered Gloria skillfully to the subject of their home.

"You must have a lovely place," he told her with a charming smile. "I'd love to see it sometime."

"Oh, by all means," Gloria said pleasantly. "Do come by some time for a visit."

Lenny was the only one at the table who saw Nick jump and stare at his wife with an expression of scarcely disguised fear.

"I just might do that," Lenny said to Gloria. "Why don't you write down the address for me—that is, if your husband doesn't mind my coming by for a visit?"

Nick blushed as they all looked in his direction. "Don't be silly," he stammered, looking down at the table. "Why would I mind?"

Gloria wrote the address down on a slip of paper and handed it to Lenny. "We're usually home," she said. "Feel free to come by any time."

Lenny folded the slip neatly and put it into his bill-fold. His eyes met Nick's, and he smiled warmly as he said, "I will, thank you, perhaps very soon."

Later that evening Lenny drove Sylvia back to her apartment; He knew, as he kissed her warmly good night, that she wanted him to come in again. The little vixen was still hot for him.

"I'd better go," he told her, stroking the softness of one thigh with his hand. At another time he might have taken advantage of her interest in him and spent the night there. As it was, however, he had other things on his mind, and he wanted the time to himself to think them over.

"I'll see you tomorrow," Sylvia said as they parted.

Lenny nodded, but the comment had given him the idea he had been looking for. He needed some time with Nick, time to break down the man's resistance. What better time than the following day, with Gloria safely at work and Nick at home by himself, writing.

He awoke bright and early the next morning, rested and in fine spirits. He drank a leisurely cup of coffee and smoked a cigarette before calling Gloria at the office.

"I'm afraid I'm a little out of practice when it comes to drinking," he told her. "Would you mind terribly if I played hooky for the day?"

"Don't be silly," she told him. "Stay home and loaf for the day, and don't worry about things here."

"You're an angel," he said, his voice taking on a more intimate tone.

"I've been called a lot of things, but never an angel," she quipped. Lenny was pleased to discover that her voice had lost that "strictly business" tone she had used with him in the past. "See you tomorrow."

When he had hung up the phone, Lenny made his way to the bathroom and shaved carefully. He shed his robe and stood looking at himself for a moment or two in the mirror. He was pleased with his looks, and admittedly vain about them. They had done all right by him in the past, and he was confident that they would serve him just as well in the future.

He showered, standing for a long time under the harsh stream of water. He emerged, finally, drying himself briskly with a large towel, and went back to the bedroom to dress. A short time later he was on his way.

The Denning home was everything that he had imagined. It wasn't, of course, palatial, but it was a large, splendid-looking place that gave every evidence of money and good taste. Lenny found himself studying it as though he were a prospective buyer, and the house were being offered for sale. Why not, he thought confidently as he mounted the steps to the front door. "After all, if everything goes well, I may be moving in here before long."

There was a long moment of silence after he rang the doorbell. He was just reaching out to ring it again when the door opened, and Nick Denning appeared in the opening. He saw Nick blush, and he realized that Nick must have expected him.

"Hi," Lenny said cheerfully, giving Nick the benefit of a radiant smile. "I'm playing hooky today."

"I know," Nick answered, trying to return the smile but failing miserably. "I talked to my wife on the phone, and she said you hadn't come to work."

It was obvious that Nick was being torn in two by the emotions raging within him. He avoided looking into Lenny's eyes, and he hadn't moved from the doorway at all except to shift his weight nervously from one foot to the other.

"Well, aren't you even going to invite me in?" Lenny asked finally.

"Oh, of course," Nick replied, almost jumping off the ground at the question. He stepped quickly backward, allowing Lenny to walk into the large front hall. "The living room is in here," he said, pointing toward an open archway.

Lenny walked ahead of him into the living room,

his quick eyes taking in the interior of the place. It was nicely furnished, a well managed mixture of various styles and periods.

"Your wife did a good job on decorating the place," Lenny commented.

"I did the decorating," Nick corrected him, then blushed again as Lenny lifted an eyebrow slightly. "It's a hobby of mine."

They stood just inside the room, facing one another. Lenny wondered for a moment whether he should make a pass just now, but he decided instead to move a little more slowly.

"You know," he said, not waiting for an invitation to be seated, "you could offer me some coffee or something."

"There isn't any made," Nick told him, remaining where he was. "I suppose I could make some..."

"No, let it go," Lenny decided, waving away the suggestion. "Let's just sit and chat for a while."

Nick started toward a chair facing the sofa on which Lenny was seated. "Not there," Lenny said, enjoying the game of cat-and-mouse he was playing with the distressed man. "Sit over here, beside me." He patted the cushion of the sofa beside him.

Nick hesitated for a moment, looking genuinely frightened at the suggestion. In the end, however, he did as Lenny had suggested, coming to the sofa to seat himself stiffly at one end of it.

"You'd think I have leprosy or something," Lenny quipped. He moved boldly closer, one strong arm coming gently about Nick's shoulders. "I'm really quite harmless, you know."

To his delight, he found that Nick was trembling beneath his arm. Lenny pulled him gently closer, excitedly aware of the effect he was having on his companion. Nick's head drooped backward against his arm, the eyes closed. He was waiting, Lenny thought gleefully, to be kissed.

"Your wife said you had a pool," Lenny said, enjoying the look of shock on Nick's face as he opened his eyes. "Why don't we go for a swim?"

"I...I should be working," Nick stammered, embarrassed by his position of surrender. He tried to meet Lenny's eyes, but the challenge was too great for him, and he looked away again. "I suppose we could for a while."

"I'll have to borrow a suit," Lenny said, standing so abruptly that he left Nick lying in a rather foolish position in the sofa. "Got one that will fit me?"

"I don't know...I suppose so," Nick commented. He started to examine Lenny's body, and blushed again. "I'll see what I can find."

Not wanting to give him a respite, Lenny followed him out into the hall and down the hall to the bedroom. Nick rummaged through a drawer of the dresser and came up with a pair of faded blue trunks, which he handed to Lenny.

"You can dress in the guest room, across the hall," Nick said.

Without argument, Lenny took the suit and crossed

the hall, leaving the doors open. He undressed quickly, listening to the sounds from across the hall that told him Nick was changing also. Lenny put his clothes carefully in the closet, slipped out of his tee shirt and shorts, and tossed the bathing suit on to the bed. Stark naked, he left the room and went back across the hall to the master bedroom.

Nick had just stepped out of his own shorts, straightening up as he heard Lenny step into the room. He was as naked as Lenny, his slender body turning almost as red as his face.

Lenny reached for the pack of cigarettes on the dresser and lit one before crossing to the bed and dropping himself down upon the surface. He lay boldly exposed to view, fully aware that Nick's eyes were glued to him. Nick had made no attempt to continue his dressing.

"There's no hurry about swimming, is there?" Lenny asked, one hand dropping invitingly to his bare thigh. "Why don't we relax for a while, okay?"

Nick was no longer capable of speaking intelligibly. He only continued to stand and stare at the nude beauty sprawled across the bed before him.

Nick moved as though he were hypnotized, advancing slowly toward the bed. It would have been impossible to hide his state of physical excitement, nor did he even seem to be aware of the matter. He lowered himself slowly to the bed, seated on one edge.

"Come on," Lenny told him coaxingly, extending one hand invitingly toward him. "It'll be all right, don't worry."

"I think you'd better go," Nick managed to whisper hoarsely.

Lenny chuckled, stubbing out his cigarette in an ashtray. "I don't think you mean that," he said, reaching for Nick. Nick tried to hold back, but it was only a weak and unspirited attempt. Lenny was pulling him down on to the bed, pushing him gently but firmly backward.

Lenny saw the eyes close again and he realized that Nick was beginning to cry softly as he lowered his face toward Nick's Their lips met. For a brief time Nick was limp and cold, but as Lenny's tongue did its magic, he began to respond, and the passion that he had been fighting raged out of control within him. Beneath Lenny's strong, hard body, Nick began to squirm and wriggle, his desire becoming more painfully obvious.

"Oh God," he moaned as Lenny's hands sought for him, coaxing him on to greater heights of desire. "Oh God!"

"It's okay baby," Lenny crooned in his ear, gradually stripping away the remnants of fear and inhibition. "I'll take care of everything. Just relax and enjoy yourself."

He was gentle at first, but as Nick's arms clung to him with ever increasing passion, Lenny became more and more savage and violent, crushing away the innocence and purity that had been Nick's, violently determined to make a sexual slave of the man beneath him on the bed.

When it was over, Nick lay with his head buried in

his arms, sobbing quietly in anguish. Lenny lay beside him, tenderly stroking the limp body until Nick's breathing grew more relaxed. Finally, Nick fell asleep.

Lenny rose from the bed, making his way back across the hall to the guest room where he had left his clothes. He stretched contentedly, pausing to admire his own reflection in the mirror. He felt good. Nick's virginity had become another trophy in his collection, and that was always pleasant. More important, however, it had all been quite easy. Nick had been perfectly ready for it to happen, and everything had gone just the way Lenny wanted it to go. From here on, it would take only a short time to have Nick eating out of his hand, too far along the road to homosexual abandon to ever turn back. Once that time came, he had only to give Nick a good shove on his way, and he would be free to work on Gloria Denning. If she was as easy to manage as her husband, he would be living in style in no time.

CHAPTER NINE

Lenny spent the rest of his day quietly, enjoying a pleasant dinner by himself that evening. He arrived at work the following morning in fine spirits, whistling happily as he made his way through the offices.

"You sure sound like you're on top of the world," Sylvia greeted him as he arrived at his desk. "That day off seemed to do a great deal for you."

"It certainly did," he told her, wondering what she would think if she knew just how his day had been. "I hope I didn't leave you with too much to handle."

"Don't worry about that," she answered with a wink. "I've never had more than I could handle."

"I can believe that," he responded, taking a quick look up and down her body. He was just wondering how soon he could arrange another session with her when Gloria Denning emerged from her office, giving him a pleasant smile.

"My husband said you were by to see him," she said, pausing at his desk.

Lenny's heart jumped. Surely Nick hadn't been fool enough to confess everything to his wife? For that matter, Gloria was no fool—what if she had guessed the truth?

"Hope you didn't mind," he said, forcing himself to sound nonchalant. "I'm afraid I interrupted his writing."

Gloria gave him a rather strange look, then smiled once again. "As a matter of fact," she said quietly, casting a quick glance at Sylvia who had directed her attention away from them. "I'm rather glad that you did. Nick's rather a shy type, as you've noticed. He doesn't make friends easily, but I think he needs someone like you for a friend—someone to bring him out of that shell he lives in. He didn't say much, but I think he enjoyed your visit—he seemed so—oh, I don't know, so relaxed last night."

"In that case," Lenny replied, barely able to suppress a laugh, "I'll have to do it again—but not on company time, of course."

She left, on her way through the office, and Lenny seated himself at his desk, smiling to himself. This was even better than he had thought. Nick's wife was actually encouraging an affair between them, without ever suspecting the truth about the relationship. Things were certainly working in his favor for a change.

When his lunch time came, he knew exactly what he would have to do. He locked his desk neatly, slipped into the jacket of his suit, and hurried to his car in the parking lot. If he drove fast enough, he would have time enough during his lunch period to visit Nick again. He didn't want Nick to have too much time to think about what had happened or determine that it wouldn't happen again.

When he answered the door, Nick looked haggard and not at all well, as though he hadn't slept at all since the day before.

"Hello again," Lenny greeted him. "I had to see you today."

Nick held tightly to the half open door, blocking the entrance to the house. "I don't think you'd better come in," he said, his voice stubbornly firm.

Lenny smiled, pleased to see the firmness of Nick's stance waver slightly. "You don't really mean that, you know," he said softly. His hand went to Nick's, pulling it slowly away from the door knob. Still holding Nick's hand, he went through the door. The door closed softly behind them as he caught Nick in his arms, pulling the weakly resisting man to him.

"No, don't," Nick sobbed, trying suddenly to struggle free of the embrace. "I won't do that again."

"Who are you kidding?" Lenny snapped, the smile fading as his eyes flashed hotly with anger. "You wanted that as badly as I did—you've been queer all along and you've just never had the guts to face it, and no one has ever made you do anything about it before I came along. But don't give me any of that precious innocence."

He was still holding Nick tightly in his arms. Nick's eyes were wide with horror, but he had ceased to struggle.

"Admit it," Lenny insisted, pulling Nick even closer. "You loved it, didn't you? No one has ever given you that sort of pleasure before have they?"

Nick's voice sobbed "No," helplessly. He offered no protest as Lenny led him down the hall, toward the bedroom at the end.

"Now I'll show you what a man is really like," Lenny said, flinging Nick down on the bed. He ripped Nick's clothes from him, not caring about the shredded fabric or the buttons that clattered noisily across the floor. He took Nick with the vicious brutality that had been his trademark in the past, not caring how much he hurt his victim, oblivious to the sobs of pain and anguish.

When he was done, he stood over the weak, helpless figure on the bed. "From here on," he snarled, wishing that he dared give the man the beating he wanted to administer, "you'll do as I tell you, okay?"

From the bed Nick nodded his head silently, his eyes closed.

"Tell your wife you've invited me to come visit you for the day Saturday." At that Nick's eyes came open, but when he saw the threatening violence on Lenny's face, he only nodded again weakly.

Lenny knelt down beside the bed, his voice suddenly gentle and soothing again. "Don't worry about it, baby," he crooned, taking Nick tenderly into his arms. "It'll be okay, just leave it to me."

He heard Nick sob again, but the slender arms came about him, and Nick was clinging to him desperately. "Anything you say," he whispered faintly.

CHAPTER TEN

Saturday arrived, and Lenny made his way to the Denning home in high spirits. He had broken Nick's will, and he was sure that Nick would soon cease to offer any resistance to any orders that he gave. Once he had completely drained Nick of any will, it would be time to toss Nick aside and concentrate on Gloria.

Too bad, he thought as he drove through the Saturday traffic. Nick wasn't a bad sort, except for his lack of backbone. No doubt he had been actually happy with Gloria—she was as strong-minded and domineering as Nick was timid and retiring. Things would certainly change when Gloria was his—he'd have to see to it that she found out who was boss. It would even be fun, in fact, to have someone who offered him a bit of a challenge. There was no doubt in his mind that he could break her down as he had everyone in the past, but it would take some doing, and he was looking forward to the fight, savoring the period of time in which he would overpower her, push her down until she was submissive to his will, a slave to his whims

The fact that Nick would have to pay for all of this didn't really bother him. After all, *he* had done his share of paying, as a kid. *He had suffered for everyone else's whims and desires, and whatever he could get now, he had coming to him!* In his mind, it was a question of kill or be killed, and he was determined to stay on top of the heap.

Nick looked awful. Lenny was positive that the man had had no sleep to speak of, and the fear and tension in his face were all too plain. If Gloria had noticed it, however, she seemed to have dismissed it without connecting it to Lenny. She was as charming and gracious as ever, even more so in fact.

"It's great to have you here," she told him as he came into the house. "Things have been so hectic lately that we haven't had much company, I'm afraid."

"Well, I'll try to live up to your welcome," Lenny told her, pleased to see that his charm was having its effect on her, melting some of her reserve at last.

"Would you like some coffee?" Nick's voice, as he asked the question of Lenny, was almost a whisper, his eyes plaintively searching Lenny's face for some notice the way a hungry dog begs from the table.

"Sure, I'd love some," Lenny answered, deliberately remaining cool and indifferent toward Nick. He watched as Nick poured the coffee from the pot.

"You know," he said, on a cruel impulse. "You're not looking well, Nick."

Nick jumped, the coffee cup rattling in his hands. "I haven't been sleeping well," he mumbled, avoiding Lenny's gaze as he set the coffee on the table.

"He's been working too hard," Gloria explained for

him. "I'm glad that he hasn't been doing too much this week."

Lenny suppressed a grin. If Nick wasn't doing much writing, it was because he wasn't able to, because he had something else on his mind. *Me,* he told himself smugly.

"It isn't such a good thing," Nick argued petulantly. "It's bad for a writer to just forget about his work. It's just that I can't seem to—oh, I don't know." He waved away the conversation with a brush of his hand.

For the rest of the morning, Lenny devoted the bulk of his attention to Gloria. He could see Nick's reaction grow from hurt disappointment to childish annoyance, but he was enjoying the game far too much to care what Nick felt or thought.

At Gloria's suggestion, they decided to go for a swim. Gloria and Nick went to their bedroom together to change, leaving Lenny no opportunity to torment Nick with his naked body. He took the suit that Gloria brought him and went to the guest room to change.

They were already at the pool when he came out. He caught the quick, admiring glance that Gloria threw at him, and he saw Nick swallow several times as he tried to tear his eyes from Lenny's body. The suit, an old one of Nick's, was several sizes too small for Lenny, and as a result it left little to the imagination. Lenny's hard, masculine beauty was displayed so blatantly that he might as well have been naked, and he took advantage of every opportunity to pose himself temptingly before the couple. He knew that Nick was almost beside himself with desire, and having a difficult time keeping the desire from showing itself. More important, however, Lenny was certain that Gloria was finding him just as appealing.

"How's the water," Lenny asked, directing his question to Gloria as he had throughout the morning. Without waiting for an answer, he ran and dived into the clear, sparkling water, swimming the length of the pool easily in strong, graceful strokes. From the time he had first begun to think of his body as an asset, and treat it as such, he had utilized swimming as an ideal exercise, with the result that he was an extremely fine swimmer. He swam back and forth several times, giving them ample opportunity to admire his skill.

"Hey, you can't just sit there and do nothing," he called to Gloria, splashing a handful of water on her feet. She jumped as the cold water hit her bare skin.

"You'll be sorry for that," she warned him with a laugh, jumping up from the chair in which she was reclining. "I may drown you."

She was a good swimmer herself, and Lenny found himself admiring her all the more as the two of them cavorted happily in the pool. Nick remained where he was, lying in the sun, watching the two of them resentfully. He declined Gloria's invitation to join them, and finally, after about an hour, he got up and lit himself a cigarette.

"I think I'll go change," he said coldly. "It's a little warm out here in the sun."

They watched him walk across the patio and into

the house. "I'm afraid Nick isn't in very good spirits," Gloria apologized with real concern in her face. "I'm a little worried about him frankly."

"It's probably not anything important," Lenny assured her, clambering up out of the pool. "Anyway, he's right, the sun is getting pretty warm. Think I'll change too."

"Make yourself at home," she called to him as he started across the patio. "I think I'll stay out a while. I need to loosen up a few muscles anyway."

Lenny let himself into the house and into the hall that led toward the bedrooms. The door to the master bedroom was closed. Without knocking, Lenny opened it and stepped inside, closing it behind him.

Nick was half in and half out of his trousers. He gave Lenny a startled look that turned to one of anger. "I think your clothes are in the guest room, across the hall," he snapped.

"It wasn't my clothes I was after," Lenny told him. He caught his thumbs in the elastic at the waist of his swimming suit, tugging it downward, over his lean hips, watching Nick with a smug smile on his lips. He saw Nick's anger begin to fade as the suit came downward and fell finally to the floor. In place of the anger there was now only hungry lust, mixed with fear and even humiliation.

He stood frozen as Lenny came slowly across the room toward him. "We can't," he begged, trying to shake his head no. "Gloria's here, she might come in."

Lenny's hand came out like lightning, slapping

brutally across Nick's face. Nick staggered backward, dropping his trousers, and fell clumsily across the surface of the bed.

"I'll tell you when, and where," Lenny told him in a low menacing voice as he came to the bed. Nick's face was crimson where the hand had struck, and his eyes were filling with tears.

"Don't make me do it again, please," Nick pleaded with him, but the rest of the plea was lost as Lenny's body crushed against his.

CHAPTER ELEVEN

When Lenny had finished, he left Nick lying on the bed and crossed the hall to the guest room, leaving the door just slightly ajar. From across the hall he heard the sounds, finally, of Nick getting up and dressing. Lenny reclined on the bed, smoking a cigarette contentedly.

Gloria came into the house just as Nick was leaving the bedroom. "I have to go out for some cigarettes," he heard Nick say, and a moment later the front door closed after him.

Lenny listened to the soft sound of Gloria's footsteps as they came down the hall and entered the bedroom, the door going gently closed. He thought of Gloria, her ripe, luscious body spilling out of the skimpy bathing suit she wore, and he imagined how she looked removing it.

"Hell," he thought suddenly, crushing out his cigarette in the ashtray. "Why imagine?"

He crossed the hall quietly and burst into the bedroom. "Nick, I...," he started to say as he appeared in the door, then stopped.

His timing had been perfect. Gloria whirled about to face him, the massive globes of her breasts bouncing as she turned. She stood completely naked at the corner of the bed, her damp bathing suit lying on the floor nearby, a towel dangling in one hand. Her eyes were wide as she saw Lenny's naked body before her.

"I thought you were still outside," Lenny lied, making no attempt to cover his nakedness. His eyes feasted on her own naked loveliness, the milk-white orbs of her breasts still jiggling, the gently rounded surface of her stomach and the patch of gold that drew the eye to her thighs.

She was breathing deeply, her eyes glued to his. He half smiled as he took a step forward, his body responding rapidly to the thoughts churning through his mind. His arms came out, drawing her to him, and she melted against him hungrily.

This is something, he thought as his mouth found hers. Husband and wife, on the same bed, within a matter of minutes.

She groaned as he found her breasts with his mouth. His hands kneaded the soft flesh of her buttocks, feeling the warmth rising within her. She might love her husband, but it was for sure that he wasn't man enough for a hot blooded vixen like her. She needed a real man, a man like him.

"I've *got* to have you," he whispered, dragging her to the bed. "I've got to have you now."

She was alive beneath him, a wild creature churning and thrashing about with only one purpose, to satisfy the lust raging within her body. She whimpered as he came into her with brutal ferocity, his body lunging downward against hers.

There was no time for gentle words or skillful play. He took her savagely and hurriedly, his mouth and his hands urging her along with him until he knew that she was ready, breathlessly eager for the frenzied wave of joy that swept over and through them.

He stood quickly, helping himself to a cigarette. "Better finish dressing," he told her, looking her over smugly. She was a tiger, all right, but he was more than enough man for her. This time had been too quick, too frantic, but he knew that she would want it again, and again. Soon, very soon, all that blonde beauty would be his, to do with as he wished.

"We shouldn't have done that," she said, getting up and reaching for the towel she had dropped. She wrapped it quickly about herself.

"Don't be silly," he told her with a smirk. "You're all woman, and I'm all man. It was bound to happen, and don't try to tell me you're sorry about it."

"You're a cold one," she said, giving him a funny look. "I don't think you would have cared if Nick had been in the house."

No more than I cared where *you* were when I was there on the bed with Nick, he thought wryly. He shrugged, and started to leave the room.

"By the way," he added, pausing at the door. "How does it feel to have a real man, for a change."

She flushed angrily. "We'd better get one thing straight," she snapped, her voice rising. "I'm sorry about what just happened, but it's over and done with.

You're probably right, I did want you—but Nick is my husband, and whatever you might think about me, I do love him, and I'm quite happy with him. This will never happen between us again."

Lenny only smiled, and left the room, returning to the room across the hall. She'd change her tune soon enough. The time would come, and it wasn't far away, when she would beg him to make love to her again. She had never had anyone who was as much a man as he was, and she wasn't likely to find another. She had had a taste of real sex, and she'd never be happy without it again. As for Nick, and her love for him—that would hardly matter when he had taken Nick from her and sent him on his way. Then she wouldn't have *any* man, and he was all too sure of which one she would want to replace her husband.

CHAPTER TWELVE

Lenny dressed and returned to the living room of the house. Gloria was already dressed and there. She gave him a cool look as he entered the room, but the sound of Nick's car in the driveway prevented any further argument between them.

For the rest of the day, Lenny was at his charming best toward both Nick and Gloria. He was the epitome of youthful fun and innocence, and it would have been impossible to imagine that this was the same man who had sexually enjoyed both people with him that same morning. Gloria's anger gradually faded, and despite herself she was soon laughing and enjoying herself again. Even Nick began to relax somewhat in the glow that Lenny was radiating.

Only at dinner did Lenny allow himself to tease them both a little. They sat at the small table in the dinette, one of them on either side. His long legs spread apart, Lenny managed to continually rub Nick's legs on his left, and Gloria's on his right, enjoying their blushes and the embarrassed way in which they tried to prevent one another from realizing what was going on. He dropped one hand to his lap and, when

Gloria wasn't looking, squeezed Nick's knee playfully, evoking a quick poke from Nick's shoe. A short time later he had the opportunity to give Gloria's knee the same treatment. She shot him a cold, angry look that almost made him laugh aloud.

"I guess I'd better call it a day," he announced finally after dinner. He stood and stretched lazily. It was still reasonably early, but then he had had a busy day.

"By the way," he said as they walked with him to the door. "I'm playing poker with some of the fellows tomorrow night, and I asked Nick to join us. I hope you don't mind."

Nick gave him a startled glance, but he recovered before Gloria had time to see it and realize that Nick knew nothing about the invitation.

"Not in the least," she answered. "I've tried to encourage Nick to get out and relax occasionally. I think it will do him good to have a night out with the boys."

That's exactly what I have in mind for him, Lenny thought, but he didn't say it aloud. "See you at seven, then," he said to Nick, confident that Nick wouldn't give anything away. Nick was already hooked, and regardless of how much he might hate what he was doing, he was already in too far over his head to resist now. Nick would be ready the following evening at seven.

* * * * * * *

And Nick was. Lenny arrived slightly after seven, and Nick was waiting nervously for him in the living room.

"Where's your wife?" Lenny asked as Nick got a sweater from the closet in the hall.

"She's in the den," Nick informed him, glancing about anxiously as though he expected Gloria to be hiding somewhere watching them. "Working on some papers from the office. She said to tell you hello."

They rode through the city in silence, Lenny paying little attention to his companion. Nick was in a bad mood, he knew, but he really didn't care. The more unhappy Nick was, the easier he would be to manage.

"Where are we going?" Nick asked finally, looking curiously out of the car window.

"You'll see."

"I told Gloria I'd be home about ten," Nick said. His tone made it almost a question instead of a statement.

"Don't count on it," was Lenny's reply. Nick made no protest.

They passed through a rather seedy section of town. Lenny turned a corner into a side street and parked the car at the curb. "I think this will do for a start," he said, climbing out of the car on his side.

His surprise was a deliberate move on his part, intended to destroy whatever might be left of Nick's self respect or self control. The bar toward which he was leading Nick was one that he knew to be "gay," a hangout for the homosexuals of the city. Surrounded by faggots, he was sure that it would not be difficult to convince Nick that he was hopelessly gay himself.

The bar was dimly lit and rather dingy. Although

it was still early, there was already a crowd inside. Young men of all types and descriptions moved about or leaned on the long bar, eyeing one another hungrily. Most of the people in the place turned to look as Lenny and Nick walked in. Lenny strutted, enjoying the admiring glances that he was getting, knowing that everyone in the place, without exception, was wishing to possess him.

Nick seemed puzzled, and then upset by the place. "Is this place a hangout for homosexuals?" he asked finally.

Lenny nodded his head and smiled. "I thought it was time you saw how your people live."

"I don't like it here," Nick told him, trying without success to sound firm.

"You will," Lenny assured him. He ordered drinks for them, handing one to Nick. "Have a drink, and relax for a change."

Nick took the drink, gulping it down much faster than was ordinary for him. Far from relaxing, however, he seemed to grow more nervous and uncomfortable as the evening went along.

Lenny, on the other hand, was enjoying himself immensely. He had only half finished his drink when someone had sent him another. Scarcely anyone passed by where he was standing at the bar without letting one hand brush furtively against his thigh. He was the center of attention, and he loved it.

It was two hours later when Lenny finally suggested that they go. Nick's relief, however, was short lived, for they drove a few blocks further on and stopped at another such bar.

"I should be going home soon," Nick offered meekly. He was already staggering from the unaccustomed drinking.

"When I say so," Lenny told him curtly, giving him a look that silenced any further argument. This bar was not much different from the other, and again Lenny very quickly became the center of attention.

Nick was getting quite drunk, and Lenny was ignoring him for long periods of time while he talked and flirted with the young men who kept coming by and starting conversations with him. Any other time he would have been trying to pick someone up, to make some money, but tonight he had other things on his mind—Nick, primarily, and plans for his companion.

By midnight he was convinced that Nick was drunk enough to do anything he said. It was time for the rest of his plans to be put into effect. He had known that seeing the crowds of homosexuals in these places would be a painful blow to Nick's morale, but he had no intention of stopping there. He wanted to make Nick wallow in the gutter, a perfect fool, and the bar wasn't the right place for that. He had made up his mind to take Nick to a gay party, the sort of wild affairs that were common to these groups.

Finding a party was no problem. There were always several scheduled, he knew, and there were any number of people in the bar who were more than willing to invite him along, with or without Nick. A short time later they were in the car again, on their way to an address not too far distant.

"I don't want to go," Nick pleaded from his side of the car. The fresh air had helped sober him up slightly, enough for him to comprehend where they were headed. "All those people they—they were awful. I can't believe anything like that is in store for me."

"Another month or so, and you'll be one of them," Lenny told him cruelly. "Hanging around in places like that, eager for any man who'll take you to bed with him."

The silence was broken by the sound of Nick's sobs.

CHAPTER THIRTEEN

The party was in full swing when they got there. It was taking place in a large, old house that had once been very elegant but had suffered badly from the passing of time. To all appearances the house was dark when they arrived.

"Looks like we've got the wrong place," Nick commented, hopefully.

"You didn't expect a neon sign, did you?" Lenny asked sarcastically. Without hesitation he led the way up the wide front steps to the door and rang the bell. A moment later the door opened a crack and a sullen face could be seen peering out. Once the man was assured that they were there rightfully, he stepped back and allowed them to enter the house.

There was good reason why the house had appeared dark when they approached. There was little enough light inside, only what was supplied by an occasional red bulb that glowed ominously. Heavy drapes over the windows prevented any of the dim glow from being seen outside, and served also to contain the noise of the party within.

From the hall they entered what had once been a

large parlor. The room was now dominated by a crude bar set up at one end where a swarm of men could be seen standing. The rest of the room was filled with moving figures, some of them dancing to the music from an unseen phonograph, others just milling about.

Lenny sensed Nick's instinctive withdrawal, and he put one arm firmly about Nick's shoulders, piloting the man through the crowd toward the bar, where they were both quickly supplied with cold bottles of beer.

"I think we should dance," Lenny said after a few moments' perusal of the room.

"I've never danced with a man before," Nick protested meekly.

"You hadn't done a lot of things with a man before," Lenny reminded him, setting his beer down on the bar. "Before you met me, that is."

Without waiting for consent, he took Nick's arm and led him out to the dance floor, joining the mass of bodies there. He held Nick's slender, trembling body pressed tightly to his own, half leading, half dragging his partner about the room.

"Relax," he insisted, holding Nick even more firmly.

"I can't," Nick whined. "I want to go."

"Later," Lenny snapped gruffly. They finished the dance and started back toward the bar.

"Well, so you're back in circulation." The voice came from behind them. Lenny stopped and looked back to see a young man that he had met in the past when he had been hustling regularly.

"More or less," he answered noncommittally. The

stranger was not the sort that he liked to mingle with, definitely low class and pretty unattractive.

"This one yours," the newcomer asked, nodding his head in Nick's direction.

Lenny smiled slightly. He intended to degrade Nick in every way possible, and this was as good an opportunity to start as any other.

"Not really," he said offhandedly. "Why, do you want him?" He ignored the shocked look on Nick's face.

"Could be," their companion declared, casting a hungry eye over Nick's body. "How about a dance?"

"I don't think so," Nick stammered, blushing with embarrassment and anger.

"Don't be a dolt," Lenny told him gruffly. "Dance with him, he's a friend of mine."

Nick gave him a hurt look, but he offered no protest as the man took his arm and led him back to where the crowd was dancing.

Lenny returned to the bar by himself and retrieved his beer, smugly watching the two dance. Nick was miserable, but he was fast losing all resistance to the way of life Lenny was presenting to him. With his resistance, he was also losing all self respect and confidence in himself as a man. It would be a simple matter now to push him over the brink into the dark pit of homosexuality, a trap from which he would never be able to return.

Nick returned a few dances later, approaching the bar glumly.

"Where's your new friend?" Lenny wanted to know.

Nick shot him a look that indicated he wanted to say several things, but apparently thought better of them.

"He had to go to the bathroom," he answered crisply. "I declined his invitation to join him."

Lenny suppressed a frown. Nick wasn't yet as completely broken as he had thought. He might give in to Lenny's demands, but he was not yet ready to submit to anyone else.

The music from the phonograph ended abruptly, leaving numerous couples standing awkwardly about the room. An elderly man, effeminate and flagrantly homosexual, appeared in the center of the room, waving his hands over his head.

"All right, girls," he squealed, his voice unpleasantly high. "Max has consented to entertain us. Everybody find a place to park it, and hold on to your wigs."

There was much laughter and commotion. Some of the guests, like Lenny and Nick, seemed puzzled by the announcement, while others exchanged excited comments about the entertainment that was in store for them.

It took a few minutes to clear the center of the room, the people crowding together in a circle. Standing as they were at the bar, Lenny and Nick had a grandstand view of the "arena" that had been provided. The center of the room was lighted now by a dim spotlight that cast eerie shadows on the faces watching expectantly.

The music began again, but this time it was not the catchy dance tunes that had been playing before. It began as little more than a whisper of sound that could scarcely be heard although the room was hushed in silence. As the volume of music increased, the plaintive melody was joined by a throbbing, insistent rhythm so suggestive as to be physically stimulating.

A door opened near the bar, and a slender figure emerged from it, pausing before he moved gracefully and lightly out into the light.

Even Lenny joined in the gasp that rose from the audience. Max was unquestionably a beautiful young man, and in this strange setting he might almost have been some young god of evil as he moved slowly about the circle in time to the music. He wore what was little more than a tunic of white, his bare limbs glistening mysteriously in the light. His eyes were nearly closed, and his face expressionless.

The audience watched in stunned silence as he began to dance, his body twisting and turning with the music. His movements became more pronounced and faster as the music gradually changed.

The tunic went in one quick movement, disappearing across the room into the crowd.

The taut, slender body was naked now except for a skimpy loin cloth that dangled in front and behind. The dance had become a frenzy of motion and liquid grace, the back arching, head swaying, limbs twisting into unbelievable positions. The piece of cloth swung and swayed, revealing brief glimpses of still more naked flesh beneath. His buttocks, molded globes of white flesh, gleamed brazenly, only to disappear again behind the fabric. No one in the room spoke or laughed.

There was no sound but the music, loud and blaring now, and the sound of heavy breathing as the spectators watched in utter fascination.

The music was building now to a frantic crescendo. The dancer crouched, his eyes opening wide. Then, with a frantic lunge, he leaped toward the bar, toward the spot where Lenny and Nick were standing. He poised, as though in mid-flight, and a murmur of awe swept around the room. The loin cloth was gone now.

The music came to a crashing end, and for a moment the room was flooded with brilliant light. The dancer paused for a second, then turned and darted lithely from the room. Lenny let out his breath, realizing suddenly that he had been holding it for longer than he remembered. He glanced at Nick. The eyes were still wide with horror, the thin face ashen white.

The lights dimmed again and a roar of appreciation went up from the room. The crowd began to move again, although no one attempted to dance. They were still all too enraptured by the performance they had just witnessed.

Someone approached, and Lenny looked up to find himself facing Max, the young dancer. Max had donned a robe of black silk that clung to his body and boldly announced the fact that there was nothing under it but naked flesh. Max was looking straight into his eyes and smiling.

"That was quite a show you put on," Lenny told him, returning the smile.

"I'm glad you enjoyed it," Max answered, puffing

lazily on a cigarette. "I was hoping that we might persuade you to entertain for a while."

"There's only one thing that I'm really good at," Lenny said, flattered by the compliment. He was aware that the others about them were watching and listening with unconcealed interest, several of them hopefully admiring his body.

"I'm sure we'd all love a demonstration," Max insisted. "Perhaps you and your friend could give us a few pointers."

Lenny glanced at Nick and saw the terror in his companion's eyes. He grinned and shrugged nonchalantly. "Sure, why not," he declared. He set his beer on the bar again and began to unbutton his shirt.

"You're crazy," Nick protested in a low voice, trying to avoid the staring eyes. Everyone in the room was watching them by this time, waiting for this next show to begin.

"Take off your clothes," Lenny told him, still smiling although his voice had taken on a new, menacing tone.

"I can't," Nick argued, his eyes filling with tears.

"Do you want *me* to take them off," Lenny whispered, dropping his voice slightly. Nick cringed and seemed about to argue further, but his fear of Lenny's violence proved stronger than his shame. He began clumsily to remove his shirt.

For Lenny there was no such thing as modesty. He tossed his shirt over the bar and continued to undress without pause, allowing his audience time enough to admire his body as it came into view. They were admiring it, too, he knew. He was a different type from Max, but he knew too that he was as beautiful a specimen of manhood as they could hope to see. He paused for a moment in his shorts, giving them time to anticipate what was coming next, and finally slid the shorts down over his hips. A gasp of astonishment and admiration passed around the room.

Nick had stripped to his shorts and was cowering back against the bar looking helplessly down at the floor. Lenny took his arm roughly and led him out to the center, into the spotlight. He took hold of the elastic of Nick's shorts and yanked them violently downward, almost toppling Nick to the floor. The audience was amused by Nick's modesty and by Lenny's rough treatment of him.

Nick lifted his eyes to Lenny's, the tears running from them down his cheeks. "Please," he moaned desperately. "Please don't make me do this."

Lenny ignored the plea. His hands on Nick's shoulders were pushing Nick downward, forcing him to his knees. He grabbed Nick's hair brutally, pulling his head roughly forward to his waiting body.

The audience roared its approval as the act progressed, Lenny becoming more and more ruthlessly violent. Nick was like a rag doll, helplessly subservient to his demands. A burst of applause greeted the vicious climax.

Lenny stood, stretching to give them a view of rippling muscles and gleaming manhood. Nick lay limply on the floor at his feet, all but unconscious.

Lenny sneered down at him and lifted his eyes to scan the audience.

"Anybody else want him," he asked, leering grotesquely. There were some expressions of surprise from the audience, and then a fresh burst of laughter as the spectators rose to the challenge.

"Sounds like a great idea," one stranger said, stepping into the circle of light as he began to shed his clothes.

"Count me in," another said, following him.

Lenny watched with a grin as several more pressed forward, hovering over Nick's naked body like so many vultures. He turned his back on them and started back to the bar and his clothes.

"You didn't ask if anyone wanted *you*," a voice said over his shoulder. It was Max, staring hopefully into his eyes.

"Meet me in back of the house," Lenny told him, moving on before Max had time to argue the choice of location.

He dressed, ignoring the numerous stares and pats he got from the crowd. Behind him the shouts and comments told him what was happening to Nick. By the time this night was over, there would be nothing left inside Nick but loathing and hatred, no trace of independence or self respect. Nick was a beaten man.

Lenny left quietly by the front door, and circled about the house. In the back a high wall cut off the yard from the neighboring houses.

Max was there, waiting for him at the foot of the

steps that came down from the back door. Lenny approached him with a smile.

"I was afraid you weren't coming," Max greeted him. He was still wearing the robe, although it hung open now to reveal his nakedness, like white alabaster in the moonlight.

"I wouldn't have missed this for the world," Lenny told him simply. His fist came out, thudding loudly against Max's chin. The scream of terror caught in his throat and came out as a choking moan.

"Don't worry," Lenny said, his fists striking the bleeding face again and again. "I won't kill you. You'll have a long time to remember how pretty you used to be."

He continued long after Max had fallen unconscious at his feet. Finally, satisfied with the damage that he had done, he wiped his hands on the shredded fabric of Max's robe and walked calmly away, around the house again to his car.

CHAPTER FOURTEEN

Lenny arrived at work the following morning in great spirits. He had seen and heard nothing of Nick since leaving him at the party, and he was fully confident now that he had done all the damage that he could do in that direction, or that needed to be done.

Sylvia was seated at her desk beside his when he approached, whistling softly to himself.

"You're in high spirits this morning," she greeted him, her eyelashes' fluttering coquettishly.

"As a matter of fact," he told her smoothly, leaning over to brush her cheek lightly with his lips, "I was thinking about you."

The look she gave him was one of mild disbelief, tempered with the wish that his statement might be true. "And just *what* were you thinking about me?" she wanted to know.

"It wouldn't be wise to draw pictures," he quipped with a wink. "Why don't we have dinner tonight, and I'll give you a demonstration?"

There was no coy hesitation in her voice as she quickly agreed. Lenny smiled inwardly as he turned to his own desk. No one could accuse Sylvia of being hard to get, at least not as far as *he* was concerned. On the other hand, he had earned a break from his campaign, and he knew from experience that she could be a pleasant diversion.

His day went smoothly enough. He saw little of Gloria, to be sure, and when they had occasion to meet one another or discuss business, he was fully aware of her coolness toward him. She was strictly business again, as she had been at the beginning, but with a subtle difference that he was quick to note. Where before she had seemed simply unaware of his appeal as a man, she now was clearly ignoring this aspect of their relationship. She was aware of him, and obviously fighting this awareness.

His knowledge of the struggle that was going on within her gave him ammunition for his plans, and he deliberately was more charming than ever with her, giving her the full benefit of flashing smiles, sparkling eyes, and every possible opportunity for bodily contact. He would drop his hand over hers on the desk, pleased when she jumped and jerked her hand away. Standing, he would move subtly closer until his hip brushed against her, and again smile with pleasure when she blushed and moved quickly away from him. There was no doubt of the attraction that she felt for him, and there was no doubt in his mind of his ability to use that attraction to his own advantage.

It was late in the morning when Nick called him on the telephone. Lenny glanced in Sylvia's direction as he recognized the voice, but she had left her desk momentarily for a cup of coffee.

"Well, I hope you enjoyed your evening," Lenny said cruelly into the phone. "I didn't think I should drag you away from all the fun."

"How could you do that to me?" Nick asked, his voice a whine that grated unpleasantly on Lenny's ears. "You knew how miserable I was. I didn't want to do any of that, and you forced me to."

Lenny laughed derisively. "Forced you to? Come off it, all you did was whine and whimper a little, and you did nothing to prevent any of it from happening. You loved it, and we both know it. That's the life for you, Nicky baby, so why kid yourself about it."

"It isn't," Nick argued, obviously crying as he spoke. "I'm not like that. I never have been."

"What do you call all those things you've done with me," Lenny demanded, all trace of affection gone from his voice. "Don't tell me you didn't enjoy yourself with me."

There was a long pause, punctuated by muffled sobs. "That's different," Nick insisted. "I can't help that, or how I feel about you. But I don't want to be queer, like those people we met last night."

"You *are* queer!" Lenny said mercilessly. "Wake up. You weren't doing anything last night that you haven't done with me. What difference does it make whether it's me or any man off the streets?"

"I love you," Nick sobbed helplessly.

Lenny smiled and allowed the silence to linger for a moment. "I don't believe you," he said finally. "You have a wife, don't you? If you really loved me, you wouldn't ask me to continue the affair the way it is."

"You want me to leave Gloria?" Nick was astonished out of his crying.

"I'm not asking you to do anything," Lenny insisted. "I'm only telling you that I won't continue the affair between us the way it is now."

There was another long silence. Lenny knew that Nick was no longer strong enough to give him up of his own will. He was like a drug addict, hooked on something that he couldn't break away from no matter how much he hated it or himself.

"If I leave Gloria, will you let me live with you?" Nick asked. He was beaten, and Lenny knew it.

"We'll see," Lenny said quietly. "No bargains, I don't do things that way. You decide what you want, and let me know." He hung up without giving Nick an opportunity to argue the matter further.

Everything was just fine. She didn't know it yet, but Gloria would soon be a free woman, free of her husband and available for a better man—and Lenny was a better man.

His good mood continued throughout the day, despite the fact that Gloria avoided him all afternoon. Lenny left the office after reminding Sylvia of their date, and returned home, enjoying a leisurely cocktail alone. After this night, he would be finished with Sylvia. All his time and efforts would be turned toward his goal of making Gloria his.

He frowned briefly as he thought of dismissing

Sylvia. He liked her well enough, and any other time he might have continued an affair with her for a while. She was good looking, pleasant to be with, and great fun in bed. And she was obviously crazy about him.

However, she couldn't fit in with his plans. He wanted the good life, the sort of life that he could have as Gloria's husband, or at least as her lover. Perhaps later, when he had Gloria well in hand, there would be time for Sylvia. After all, he was quite capable of satisfying both of them, and he knew only too well that no one woman would ever be able to satisfy him. The prospect of having both Gloria and Sylvia at his disposal restored his smile. Two hot blooded, lovely vixens were far better than one.

"But," he reminded himself, finishing his drink and starting for the bathroom, "I don't dare risk the campaign for Gloria by continuing to court Sylvia." She would have to be put on the shelf for the present. He was certain that he could regain her affection whenever he wished in the future.

He slipped out of his robe and stood for a moment admiring himself in the mirror. No one, woman or man, would ever be able to love him quite as fully as he loved himself. There was no room for anyone else in his affections.

Other people, the men and women he used to gain his desires, were only so many tools to be employed as needed, and discarded when he was finished with them. There was no sympathy for Nick, or Sylvia, no affection for Gloria.

Not since he had been a child had he had any feeling for anyone, and that had been too long ago for him to remember. Caring for someone, anyone, was a weakness, a mistake that made one vulnerable just as Nick and Sylvia were vulnerable. So long as he cared for no one else, he would never be vulnerable. He would continue to rule the people about him with the weapons that they themselves put into his hands—their desire for his masculine beauty, and their love for him.

He was late when he arrived to pick up Sylvia, although the fact caused him no concern. If she was offended, however, he quickly dispelled any annoyance that she felt. He was sweet and pleasant toward her, treating her as though he was genuinely in love with her, giving her all the right glances and smiles, saying all the right things.

"Isn't this rather expensive?" she asked when they arrived at the restaurant, a smart Beverly Hills establishment.

"Nothing is too good for you," he told her tenderly, coming around the car to open the door for her. She blushed, pleased by the compliment.

A smartly dressed maitre d' led them to a quiet table in a dim corner of the restaurant, and Lenny ordered cocktails for both of them. They drank slowly, the conversation a succession of sweet nothings that Lenny whispered across the table to her, enjoying the glow in her eyes as she succumbed to his magic.

He ordered for them finally, ordering lavishly from the expensive menu. Tonight he was sparing no expense. Soon, he told himself, he would be amply repaid for his expenditures. With Gloria Denning's money, he would never have to worry about a budget again. He could afford to splurge now in anticipation of his new affluence.

Vast trays of hors d'oeuvres arrived, the scent of strange spices drifting up to their nostrils. The salads were crisp and flavorful, the Chateaubriand a gourmet's delight. There was champagne with the dinner, and afterwards the cherries jubilee were followed by coffee and fine cognac.

"You know," she said as she allowed him to light her cigarette for her, "you certainly know how to make a woman feel like a queen."

"Only when I'm with a queen of a woman," he said softly, looking deep into her eyes.

When they returned to the car, he headed for his own apartment. He fully intended to make a night of it. In the morning, Sylvia could be driven to her own apartment, or maybe just told to leave and find her own way home. That, he thought sadistically, would be a fine gesture with which to end the evening.

She gave him a hesitant glance as he parked the car in front of his apartment building. "Tomorrow is a working day, you know," she reminded him without any real conviction in her voice.

"Don't let that spoil tonight," he said, taking her hand in his and lifting it briefly to his lips. He helped her from the car and led the way into the building, where the small elevator carried them to the third floor.

He was glad now that he had invested the money in a nice apartment for himself. At the time it had seemed an extravagance, but he realized that it would be necessary, too, in his campaign for Gloria. She would never go for a slob, and he would need to impress her with the fact that he was the right kind of man for her, out of bed as well as in.

Once inside the apartment, he was in no hurry to get down to bare facts. He was enjoying playing the part of the romantic lover with Sylvia, a role in which he was quite skilled. He brought coffee for them, and more cognac, and they snuggled together cozily on the sofa to listen to soft music from the phonograph.

"I don't know when I've had such a wonderful evening," she sighed, leaning happily against him.

"It isn't over," he reminded her in a low voice. His hand slid under the satin smoothness of her skirt, edging its way upward over the length of silk stockings. In his arms, she trembled as his hand found its way to her warm moist thighs and the silk that encased them.

His lips sought hers, his tongue scorching its way inside her mouth, seeking and finding hers. She was weak now with excitement, her hungry young body trembling in response to his touch.

"Wait, I'll help," she whispered as he fumbled with the catch of her dress.

"I can't wait," he answered, catching the fabric firmly in his hands. The dress tore easily, ripping away to leave her body exposed and shivering beside him. She gasped, but he silenced her protests with another long, searing kiss. All of his gentleness and tenderness were gone now, and he had become a vicious beast, intent only upon satisfying the lust rising within him. He felt her wince as he ripped the bra from her, throwing it to the floor. He mauled her breasts mercilessly, and although she struggled in his arms, the nipples quivered and swelled, growing hard in his fingers.

His hand went down to the elastic of her panties, and the filmy silk offered little resistance to his feverish actions. She was naked now, a vision of creamy white flesh and gleaming black hair. His hungry mouth sought her breasts, savoring each in turn, and moved lower, kissing a white hot trail over the satin softness of her stomach to the smoldering thighs.

"I can't stand it," she cried, moaning and writhing in his grasp. With a suddenness that took her breath away, he stood, sweeping her up in his arms, and carried her to the bedroom, where he hurled her bodily to the bed. His clothes fell swiftly to a heap on the floor, and he lunged for her like a mad bull.

His hand covered her mouth, stifling her cry of pain that quickly became a moan of pleasure. He was oblivious to everything but the pounding of his body against hers, his hips rising and falling wildly, his hands clawing at the tenderness of her squirming buttocks.

"Lenny, Lenny," she sobbed, beside herself with ecstasy, clinging deliriously to his thrashing body.

The white hot fury of their act grew faster and hotter, becoming an overwhelming whirlwind of passion and lust.

"Now," she cried aloud. "Now, now!"

He let go, releasing the madness within himself. They skyrocketed to the heights of pleasure, and the room seemed to explode about them.

He became dimly aware of a bell ringing somewhere far away. It was a moment before he placed it, his own doorbell. Someone was ringing it steadily and persistently.

"Don't answer it," Sylvia pleaded beneath him, her warm young body still alive with the urgency of her need for him.

Lenny hesitated, listening to the bell. His curiosity, however, was greater than his desire for a second round with her. He sighed and rose from the bed, taking his robe from the closet and slipping quickly into it. He left her in the bedroom and crossed the living room toward the door.

CHAPTER FIFTEEN

Lenny opened the door and stepped back in surprise. Nick was standing there in the hall, a small suitcase in his hand. But it was not the same Nick that he had met a few weeks before. The thin blond man looked like a wild and frightened animal. His eyes glittered hysterically, his face pale and drawn.

"What are *you* doing here?" Lenny asked, half guessing the answer already.

"I've come to you," Nick told him. "It was what you said you wanted."

The elevator clanged in the hallway, and Lenny realized someone was coming home. He hadn't intended to invite Nick in, but he certainly didn't want to stand in the hall arguing while the neighbors went by. He stepped back into the room, allowing Nick to enter, and closed the door after him.

"What do you mean, you've come to me?" he asked, facing Nick coldly. "I told you our affair would have to end."

Nick was too desperate to be stopped by such bluntness. "You said it couldn't go on as it was."

"Well then," Lenny started to argue.

"Don't you see," Nick interrupted him, talking loudly and rapidly. "I've left Gloria."

Lenny caught his breath. He hadn't expected Nick to leave Gloria and come running to him so quickly. "You left her?"

Nick nodded his head frantically. "I told her everything, about us and that I was in love with you."

Lenny caught Nick's arm in a savage grip. *"You told her about us?"*

Nick tried to free his arm from the iron grip. "I told her I had to come to you, no matter what. I've left her, Lenny, for good."

"You fool!" Lenny spat out the words. His hand came up swiftly, slapping Nick across the face with violent fury. He hadn't counted on this, on Nick's telling Gloria about him as well.

Nick began to sob, his words running together in a desperate stream. "You said you wanted me to leave her, you said this was the life for me. I'm yours now, you can do whatever you want with me, don't you understand?"

Lenny released his grip and turned his back on Nick. He would have to see Gloria as soon as possible, convince her that there was nothing queer about him. He could make her believe that he had only submitted to Nick's demands out of sympathy.

"Why are you angry with me?" Nick sobbed from behind him.

"Get out of here," Lenny snarled without turning. "Do you think I'd want a weak, sniveling faggot like you hanging around me? You make me sick!"

Nick moaned aloud and ran to him, clinging to his back. "Don't say that," he pleaded.

Lenny struck him viciously, sending him sprawling to the floor. Without even caring if he had hurt him, he walked to the cabinet across the room and poured himself a stiff drink, downing it in one swallow. He had to think, reorganize his thoughts.

"What's this?" Nick had managed to stop his sobs for a moment. Lenny turned as Nick got up from the floor and went to the sofa, where Sylvia's tattered clothes were lying.

"What do *you* care?" Lenny snapped. He had forgotten Sylvia, in the bedroom, where she could hear everything.

"There's someone here," Nick shouted, his anger sweeping away the grief that had overcome him. He whirled about and started for the bedroom.

"Stay out of there," Lenny ordered, starting after him. They both came to a halt as Sylvia appeared in the doorway, still stark naked and obviously angry.

"You!" Nick shouted, moving as though to strike her. Lenny moved faster, grabbing his arm and half throwing him across the room.

"Get out of here!" he shouted again, his anger surging almost out of control.

For a moment Nick stared at him contemptuously. Then, without another word, he turned and dashed out of the apartment.

Lenny breathed deeply, trying to regain his self

control. Finally he turned back to Sylvia. She was fumbling with her clothes, trying to provide herself with a temporary outfit.

"I can explain all this," he told her, wondering how much trouble she might cause with Gloria.

"Don't bother," she told him coldly, pinning her torn dress shut with a brooch. "I'm leaving too."

He stood blankly as she finished dressing and walked past him briskly toward the door. A moment later the door slammed again.

"Damn!" he swore aloud. Everything had been going so well for him, and that fool of a man had made a mess of it. He had even been deprived of the pleasure of ending his affair with Sylvia.

Still seething with anger, he crossed the room and poured himself another drink, downing it as quickly as the first.

Let them go, he thought angrily. He was finished with both of them anyway, and they were no longer any good to him. As for Gloria, what did it matter how much Nick had told her. She was a woman, and she wanted him, there was no doubt in his mind of that. He would win her over, no matter what she thought of him at the moment. No one had ever been able to refuse him before.

A nagging thought crossed his mind—no one had ever walked out on him before, either, until Sylvia had done so a moment ago.

He poured another drink and pushed the thought from his mind.

CHAPTER SIXTEEN

Lenny had several drinks before he finally calmed down again. He thought for a while about going out, picking up some faggot that he could vent his anger on, but in the end he tossed the robe aside and went back to bed, where he soon fell asleep.

In his dream he was running, and after a while he saw the figure running before him. It was Gloria Denning, naked and beautiful. He pursued her relentlessly, although his body began to ache with tiredness. It was as though he were running through thick mud, scarcely able to lift his feet from the ground. He would gain on her, reach for her, but she would elude him, slipping from his grasp, and the chase went on.

He awoke drenched with sweat and tired despite the hours of sleep. He was depressed and in ill humor as he shaved and showered and made ready for the office.

"I won't let myself be thrown by a dream," he told himself stubbornly, knotting his tie. Gloria Denning would be his, and he intended to start toward that goal at once, this very day. She would be angry, and she would try to fight her desire for him, but he knew that once he had her in his arms again she would surrender to him. After that, he would have his way with her.

The office seemed strangely quiet and subdued as he entered it. No one greeted him, or seemed to be saying much to one another.

He went straight to his own desk. Sylvia was at hers, already at work. She looked up at him as he approached, and the look she gave him was one of cold hatred.

"Still angry with me," he asked, forcing a smile. "I can be a pretty nice guy, you know." He hadn't intended to try to make up with her, and yet, in some way that he couldn't fathom, he was sorry that she had walked out on him the night before.

For the first time in his life, someone else's opinion of him seemed to matter, and suddenly he wanted to restore himself to her good graces.

His smile had no effect on her. "Nick is dead," she told him crisply, her voice bristling with dislike for him.

The words stunned him, wiping the smile from his face. "Dead?" he repeated the word. "What do you mean he's dead?"

"He killed himself," she explained, still staring coldly into his eyes. "He jumped onto the freeway last night, right into the stream of traffic. There wasn't much left of him when it was over."

Lenny drew in his breath sharply and sat down at his desk. This was something else he hadn't counted on. If there had been a suicide note, or if Gloria and Sylvia brought him into it, he could be in plenty of hot water.

"Was there a suicide note?" he asked, lighting a

cigarette with trembling fingers.

"Don't worry," she answered. "You weren't implicated. I haven't said anything either, and I don't think Gloria will, if only out of respect for her husband."

"Where is Gloria now?" he asked. The moment of shock was passing, and his mind was beginning to work again. If he was going to make the grade with Gloria, it would have to be at once. If he hadn't been implicated, then Nick's suicide was no problem to him. In fact, it might well work to his advantage. Gloria would be distraught, not in full control of herself. She would need someone to cling to, someone who could relieve the grief she would be feeling.

"She had to go to the morgue," Sylvia told him. "She should be here soon. I suppose it's too much to hope that you might at least offer her an apology."

Lenny smiled again, without quite so much effort. "As a matter of fact," he lied, "that's exactly what I want to do."

It was an hour later when Gloria did appear. She had been crying, and the strain of the difficult night was showing on her. There was none of the cool assurance of polish that she ordinarily wore.

Lenny assumed an air of sympathy, studying her as she came across the office. He was certain that she would be quite vulnerable in her present condition. He stood up as she came past his desk.

"I want to talk to you," he said quickly, taking hold of her arm.

She yanked her arm away, fixing a look of loathing

on him. "Don't touch me," she snapped. "And don't ever let me see you again."

This was a crucial moment, one that he had to use to his advantage, and the tears in his eyes were genuine as he spoke.

"Please, at least give me a chance to explain and tell you how badly I feel."

She hesitated, waiting for him to go on, and he felt some of her determination weaken.

"I think we should talk in your office," he said, nodding in Sylvia's direction. He had to be alone with her, and he couldn't risk allowing her the time to multiply her anger and hatred for him.

She looked away from him, nodding her head slightly, and went on toward the door to her office. Lenny followed her inside, closing the door after them. With one hand behind him, he locked the door. He didn't want anyone disturbing them, not with what he had in mind.

"I didn't mean for this to happen," he said gently, coming toward her.

"That isn't much of an excuse," she said bluntly, moving away from him and behind her desk. "You'll have to do better than that."

"Can't you see," he went on, following her around the desk. "I did it all because I love you. I love you so much that I could stop at nothing to make you mine."

She was staring at him in wide-eyed astonishment. As she realized suddenly what was happening, she tried to move away from him again, but he was faster.

She was suddenly in his arms, his mouth seeking for hers.

"You beast," she swore at him, struggling to free herself from his embrace. "You drive my husband to suicide and then you come here trying to paw over me."

"You want me too," he told her, his hands boldly grasping at the soft, warm flesh beneath the fabric of her dress. "I know you do, admit it. I'll make you happy, you know I will."

"Let me go," she demanded, "Or I'll scream for help."

Lenny crushed his mouth over hers, holding her helplessly in his strong arms. He had hoped to subdue her anger with sweet words, but he could see it would take more than that. Once he made love to her, he was sure she would cease fighting him. He pushed her backward against the desk, bending her over it.

She struggled wildly, but she was no match for him, and her resistance only increased the lust within him. He tore at her underclothing, the silk ripping as easily as had Sylvia's the night before.

Her struggles continued, but he was aware, too, of the fact that her body was responding despite herself, quivering to his touch. She was a woman of hungry passions, and her body was starving for the sort of pleasure he had given her before. Even as she fought against him, he could sense the desire welling up in her. With her mind, even her hands, she was fighting him, but her thighs were welcoming him to her.

He took her hurriedly, sorry that he couldn't give

her the performance he would have liked. She ceased struggling, her body pinned helplessly between his and the desk, and as he urged her on to her climax an involuntary moan of pleasure escaped her lips beneath his.

He had won his case, he was sure of it. There would be time enough later to talk, to convince her of his rightness for her.

He left the office without a word, leaving her leaning silently and weakly against her desk. He closed the door behind himself and went to his own desk, gathering up his cigarettes and lighter.

"I'm taking the day off," he told Sylvia with a dazzling smile. He ignored her astonished glance and walked briskly away.

CHAPTER SEVENTEEN

It was proving to be a good day. There was no sympathy or regret in Lenny's reaction toward Nick's suicide. There had been his fear that his own plans were thwarted, but he was confident again that he would succeed with Nick's recently widowed wife.

His plans were perfectly clear. He would give the day to Gloria, allow her to consider what had happened in her office, remember the pleasure he had given her, even in the depths of her sorrow and anger.

In the evening, he would go to see her, at her home. He would make love to her as an artist, bring the fulfillment she could never hope to achieve with any other man. She would not refuse him again, of that he was certain.

The day passed pleasantly and leisurely. He had a late breakfast at the small lunch counter on the corner, and came back to his apartment. With his spirits restored, he was able to sleep pleasantly now, and this time in his dream Gloria was not running, but clinging hotly to him as he took her luscious body.

The doorbell woke him sometime during the afternoon. For a second he frowned remembering Nick's visit the night before. He remembered, then, that it could hardly be Nick this time.

Perhaps it was Gloria. Maybe he had underestimated his appeal for her. It was entirely possible that she had come to him, to beg him to take her again. With a smile on his face, Lenny donned his robe, leaving it untied, and hurried to the door.

It wasn't Gloria. Two strangers stood in the hall, huge burly men with unpleasant faces.

"You Lenny?" one of them asked in a surly voice.

Without thinking, Lenny answered "Yes" quickly. Before he could regret the admission, he was being shoved roughly aside, and the two of them were entering the apartment.

"Wait a minute," he protested, trying to block their entrance into the room. "You can't just come in here..."

He didn't get to finish his protest. A massive fist caught him solidly on the jaw, sending him reeling backward into a lamp table, which toppled over behind him. He lurched, trying to regain his balance and defend himself, but the other man was behind him, grabbing his arms in a grip like steel, and he had only a glimpse of the fist crashing down on him again before his head seemed to explode with the impact.

He fought wildly, but to no avail. Either one of them would have been a good match for him, despite his own size and brute strength. Together they were just twice as much as he could hope to handle. Savage blows rained down on him without relief, and he sank helplessly to his knees. A shoe caught him beneath the chin, toppling him over backward, and he lay only barely conscious as hands and feet pounded against him.

It seemed an eternity later. He had not even heard them go or been aware of their leaving. The apartment was silent, nothing stirring. He opened one eye cautiously, and pulled himself painfully to a sitting position. The other eye was already swollen shut, and when he touched it his hand came away messy with blood.

It was so senseless, so without reason. Why would they have done this to him, a perfect stranger? He thought of people who had received the same treatment from him in the past, but they wouldn't have known where to find him, and most of them didn't even know who he was, other than a handsome stranger in some park.

Finally he saw the envelope on the floor, dropped near where he was lying. He picked it up, the scent of perfume touching his nostrils. He knew, almost before he opened it, what it was all about.

The note was short and to the point:

"The next time, I'll have them kill you."

There was no signature, but he knew it was from Gloria.

After a long time he was able to get up and make his way to the bathroom. It wasn't a pretty sight that greeted him in the mirror. He ran water and splashed it over his face, wiping away the rapidly drying blood despite the pain it produced from several cuts.

There still wasn't much improvement. Several of the cuts were sure to leave scars, and it would take a long time for the bruises to heal. Nor was it only his face—they had inflicted as much or more damage to his body. Their intention had been plain enough—don't kill him, just mess him up badly.

He staggered back to the living room, to the open bottle of liquor. Without looking for a glass, he tipped the bottle up and drank rapidly and long from it. He had to dim the pain that he was feeling, not all of it physical.

CHAPTER EIGHTEEN

He drank until he had drained the bottle, and finally he was able to stumble to the sofa, falling weakly against it as he passed out.

It was evening when he woke up once again. The room was dark, and for a moment he couldn't remember what had happened. The memory came, then, and he sat up, aware of the ache that filled his entire body.

He had been wrong about Gloria. No, her anger toward him had only increased with what he had done, and she had taken her revenge swiftly. With her money and determination, surely it would not be hard for a woman to hire the men who had done the job for her. There had been no risk of his going to the police, either, or making trouble for her over it.

There was nothing left of his plans for her. To try again would only invite more of the same. He had no doubt that she would carry out her threat to do even worse. He had lost, even though it had all seemed to be in his favor. He had nothing, not even a job.

Suddenly, overwhelmingly, he wanted sympathy and affection from someone, someone who would hold on to him and make him feel good again. He thought of

Sylvia. What a fool he had been to toss her aside. How wonderful it would be right now to be with her, in her arms, making love to her lithe, young body.

Why shouldn't I be, he thought abruptly, sitting up to reach for a cigarette. He knew that she loved him, angry though she might have been. She had been thrilled beyond her wildest dreams by his affair with her. She hadn't lost any husband, as Gloria had done. If he went to her, apologized and begged her forgiveness, she would take him back again. She would have to!

He got up and began to clean up, a slow process with the condition of his face and body. When he had done all that he could to repair the damage, he dressed, choosing a long sleeved shirt of a soft fabric that would cover the marks on his arms without causing him too much discomfort.

There was little he could do about the cuts on his face. He grimaced at himself in the mirror. There was no point in kidding himself, he was still far from a pretty sight. With a helpless sigh, he left the apartment and went downstairs to the garage where his car was parked.

Driving was rather clumsy. He was more stiff and sore than he had realized, and he was forced to remain in the slow moving lane of traffic, piloting the car cautiously. He was able, finally, to reach Sylvia's apartment. He parked outside, sitting for several long minutes while he tried to summon his courage. He had never had to truly apologize to anyone before, and the prospect was far from a pleasant one.

What the hell, he told himself finally with stubborn determination. A few cuts and bruises couldn't erase the good looks that were normally his. Sylvia had seen him looking at his best. What's more, she knew only too well the pleasure that he could provide. One woman might be able to overlook that fact in her anger, but it was impossible that two women would be able to turn him down. He got out of the car, slamming the car door in annoyance with himself and started briskly up the walk toward the apartment building.

Despite his forced bravado, he was far from smug as he rang the bell at her door. It seemed an eternity before there was any response from within, and he half feared that she might be out, maybe for the night. His relief was immense when he heard the muted sound of footsteps inside the apartment, and a moment later the door opened.

Sylvia stood there in a clinging negligee of some almost transparent blue material. She had never looked lovelier to him, or more desirable.

"May I come in?" he asked, aware that she was only standing there looking at him, almost as though she didn't know who he was. Maybe, he thought, the face is more of a mess than I thought.

She stepped wordlessly aside and allowed him to enter the apartment, closing the door after him. Still there was no indication of hospitality or happiness to see him. Lenny tried hard to hold on to his confidence.

"What happened to you?" she asked.

The question was very business-like, strictly curiosity with no trace of concern or sympathy in her voice.

"Compliments of your boss," he admitted bluntly. There wasn't much to be gained by lying about it. "Pretty nasty, isn't it?"

She shrugged, walking past him to take a cigarette from a ceramic dish on the coffee table. "You had it coming," she said coldly, "And probably a lot more than that."

He winced, and tried unsuccessfully to force a smile to his lips. Things weren't going his way at all.

"Her loss," he said flippantly, taking the cigarette from her hand and inhaling deeply, "Your gain."

Her eyebrows lifted, but she held her words for a moment and lit herself a fresh cigarette. "My gain?" There was cold mockery in her voice. "What makes you think I'm interested?"

Lenny's heart seemed to stop for a second, but he forced himself to remain calm. She was only bluffing, making him suffer a little. She wanted him, he was sure of it, she only wanted to be coaxed a little.

"You're interested," he told her, moving closer. One arm went about her waist, holding her close to him. His hand went to her flaring buttocks, caressing them through the filmy material. "Have you forgotten what a real man is like?"

"No, I haven't," she said softly. He bent toward her, toward her full, red lips.

"I haven't forgotten what a rat is like, either," she said abruptly. She jerked free of his embrace, stepping quickly away from him. "I think you'd better go."

He stared at her in disbelief. This couldn't be happening, not to him. There wasn't a woman alive, or a man either, who wouldn't love to get him in the hay. Who was this silly broad trying to kid, turning him down this way.

"You're crazy," he told her, his voice becoming a whine without his realizing it. "I can make you happy, you know I can. And I'm all yours now, don't you understand that? Nick is gone, and Gloria's out of the picture. You won't have to share me with anybody."

"I certainly won't," she agreed curtly. "Because someone else can have my share. Can't you get it through your head, Casanova, that I'm not interested? You're a beast, a savage animal incapable of feelings for anyone but yourself. You drove Nick to suicide, and there's not a trace of remorse in you for him. God only knows what you did to Gloria besides killing her husband, but whatever it was I'm sure you earned the beating you got. I don't intend to give you the chance to destroy me. Now get out of here, and don't ever come back."

For a brief instant Lenny's eyes flashed anger, and he wanted to strike her, lash out at her and hurt her the way she had hurt him. But the moment passed, and he dropped his arms loosely at his side. What was the use—he was beaten, and he knew it.

...He turned and walked silently past her, toward the door. He kept hoping, as he moved, that she would weaken, call him back, but there was no sound from her. He let himself out, fighting down the impulse to

cry once he was in the hall. He shuffled morosely out of the building, to his car parked outside, and drove slowly away.

CHAPTER NINETEEN

"Give me another one, and make it double." Lenny pushed his glass in the direction of the bartender. He was aware that the bartender was studying him, no doubt wondering if he were too drunk to be served another one. He decided finally in Lenny's favor, and a moment later a fresh drink appeared on the bar.

Lenny swallowed a mouthful of the cheap bourbon and turned on his barstool, trying to focus his eyes on the scene. The bar was crowded, thick clouds of smoke shimmering whitely in the glow of light from the jukebox and the wall fixtures.

He didn't know where he was. There had been many bars after leaving Sylvia's apartment, and one of them was much the same as the others. This one was a dive, dirty and seedy looking. The customers looked like the dregs of humanity, and Lenny little cared.

He took another sip of his drink, and turned his head slightly toward the juke box. A couple was dancing crudely to loud music that poured from the machine. The guy was drunk, and Lenny felt a brief sensation of sympathy for the pathetic figure stumbling about the floor trying to keep up with the bouncing blonde.

His attention shifted to the girl. She was a disgusting sight, even given benefit of the bad lights and his drunken condition. Her breasts were sloppy, loose hanging pendulums that bounced and swayed with the dancing. Her hips were broad, her fanny fleshy and unshapely. Her long hair, dyed too many times, was a straggly looking mop of yellow.

There's one who wouldn't turn me down, he thought bitterly. She'd take me on, no matter what. The thought, self-humiliating though it was, gave him some odd sort of comfort. The more he watched her, the more it stayed with him, until he knew finally that he would have to prove the statement to himself. It didn't matter that she was a mess, or that any other time he wouldn't have given her the time of day. He only knew that had to prove his appeal, to anyone.

They had finished dancing, making their way clumsily back to a small table nearby. The man got up and staggered away in the direction of the restrooms. Lenny got up from his stool, swaying unsteadily, and crossed the bar toward the blonde.

"How about dancing with a real man?" he asked, flashing a smile at her.

She looked up at him blankly.

"Sure," she said without any enthusiasm. She stood and they made their way to the small dance floor, where the music was blaring again.

Lenny held her close, piloting her slowly about. He was no longer aware of any stiffness or soreness—he was too drunk to feel any physical pain.

The blonde moved drearily in his arms, her warm flesh rubbing dispiritedly against his body. Her cheap perfume mingled with the unpleasant odor of her body, and he wondered idly when she had bathed last. As though making himself suffer, he became more amorous toward her.

"Hey, you're a pretty hot one, ain't you?" she asked as his hands fondled her jiggling buttocks.

"Sure thing, baby," he whispered, almost laughing in her ear. "For *you,* anyway."

The music came to a stop, and she moved back away from him, looking up into his face. The room was dimly lighted, particularly where her table had been. Now there was the glow from the jukebox, and she saw his face for the first time. One of the cuts had bled some more, leaving an ugly trail across his forehead, and the bruises had gone violently black by this time.

"Jesus, you're a mess," she said abruptly.

Lenny stared at her in shock. It was as though she had hit him. He shook his head, anger seething up inside him.

"I'm not," he said harshly, grabbing her arm. "I'm a knockout, get that, a beautiful hunk of man!"

She stared at him puzzled for a moment. Then, quite unafraid of him, she threw back her head and laughed hoarsely.

"A nut," she howled, bringing the attention of the other customers to them. "An honest to goodness nut, that's what you are."

Lenny's anger boiled out of control. "You filthy slut,"

he shouted, striking her angrily. "You bitch, I'll teach you to laugh at me."

Her scream was followed by a roar of commotion about them. Her boyfriend was there, grabbing his arm, "What's the big idea," he demanded loudly, and Lenny saw the bartender, a burly ape of a man, shoving his way through the crowd toward them.

"He's a nut!" the girl was shouting by way of explanation to any and all questions, Lenny was shoved through the crowd, toward the door, and a minute later he landed in a heap on the sidewalk outside,

"Don't let me see you in here again," the bartender shouted as he disappeared back inside.

Lenny lay limply on the sidewalk, trying to collect his thoughts. He was washed up. He couldn't even pick up a broken down bag of a woman in a lousy bar like this one.

A dog came by, a bony looking mongrel, and sniffed suspiciously at Lenny's foot. Lenny kicked him, sending the dog on his way with a yelp of pain and fear.

"Damn them," he thought crazily. "Damn them all!"

He managed to stand up, finally, staggering awkwardly down the street. To hell with them, he'd make out. He'd pick up a faggot. Queers didn't care what you looked like as long as you had the old magic swinging. He'd find some silly faggot, with a bundle of dough, and he'd make out all right.

There was a park across the way, its dark recesses luring him toward it. He crossed the street, oblivious to the traffic lights and honking of horns that accented his progress.

He followed the sidewalk that led into the park, past the well lighted sections near the street, heading for the darkness and the safety it offered him. He passed a man on a bench, and gave him a leer, but the man didn't appear interested, so he went on into the darkness.

At last he stumbled off the walk, into cool grass. He caught at a tree, falling to his knees, and remained there for a long time, his head reeling.

Where had it all gone wrong? Lenny, with the good looks and the sex to match, he could have had anything he wanted. How had he managed to mess things up?

A patch of light flared nearby then disappeared. He knew instinctively what it was—a match. Someone was lighting a cigarette.

Sucking in his breath, Lenny forced himself to turn. A man was standing a few feet from him, smoking a cigarette and watching him. He was young, probably no older than Lenny himself, and thin. Lenny didn't have to be sober to know the guy was queer, and giving him the eye. He smiled, a rather sickening smile.

"Looks like you're having a night of it," the stranger said, encouraged by the smile to come a little closer.

"It's my birthday," Lenny told him. He managed to stand, leaning against the trunk of the tree for support.

"Why are you celebrating it alone?" the stranger asked, giving him a smile and coming still closer. They were standing together now.

For an answer, Lenny reached for the fly of his trousers. The zipper sounded harsh in the still darkness. The stranger followed the gesture with hungry eyes. He dropped his cigarette to the ground, stepping it out with one foot as he kneeled in front of Lenny.

Lenny leaned against the tree, head back and eyes closed, and breathed heavily, scarcely aware of what was happening. He was past feeling, or caring, and he hardly knew when it had ended, until the stranger tugged his zipper closed again and stood.

"Do you need some money?" the stranger asked, licking his lips nervously.

Lenny stared at him. No, it wasn't money he needed. He needed satisfaction, vengeance on the world that had treated him so cruelly. He smiled, a genuine smile.

"Come here," he whispered, crooking his finger. "Closer to me."

Puzzled, the stranger moved closer. Lenny's fist came up like a hammer, shattering the expression of concern on the strange, thin face. He caught the man's jacket, his fist striking again, and again. He wasn't tired anymore, or in pain. He had the strength of a hundred men, and he used it all, pounding the stranger into oblivion, hitting and kicking at the limp figure that was now unconscious.

It seemed to go on forever. He didn't know how much later it was when the truth dawned on him. The man was dead.

He knew it even before he kneeled and listened for the heartbeat that wasn't there. He stared at the bloody, beaten figure, feeling no pain or sympathy. He half smiled, and spat on the almost unrecognizable face.

"Hey, you there!" The voice startled Lenny from his mood of satisfaction. He looked up in time to see the policeman looming down upon him, half running.

There wasn't time to think. Lenny jumped up and started off across the damp grass, through the darkness. He heard the policeman swear behind him, and knew he had stopped at the dead body.

"Stop, or I'll shoot!"

The warning didn't even register. Lenny was an animal now, obeying animal instincts. There was only one thing to do now, and that was to run, head for safety.

Even the sound of shots meant nothing to him. He didn't even recognize them as shots, or realize that they were aimed at him. He was only dimly aware of a sudden, brief pain at the small of his back, and he seemed, suddenly to go lighter, as though his feet had wings.

He had time to realize, before he died, that he was falling, tumbling over and over in the damp, cool grass, and then the world ceased to exist for him.

ABOUT THE AUTHOR

VICTOR J. BANIS—VICTOR JAY—is the critically acclaimed author ("...a master storyteller"—*Publishers Weekly*) of more than 200 published novels and numerous shorter works in a career spanning nearly a half century. A longtime Californian, he lives and writes now in West Virginia's beautiful Blue Ridge region.

www.ingramcontent.com/pod-product-compliance
Lightning Source LLC
Chambersburg PA
CBHW050800250626
47155CB00005B/2150